THE DALLERGUT DREAM DEPARTMENT STORE

THE DALLERGUT DREAM DEPARTMENT STORE

A NOVEL

MIYE LEE

TRANSLATED BY SANDY JOOSUN LEE

HANOVER
SQUARE
PRESS

HANOVER
SQUARE
PRESS™

Recycling programs
for this product may
not exist in your area.

ISBN-13: 978-1-335-08117-9

The Dallergut Dream Department Store

Hanover Square Press
22 Adelaide St. West, 41st Floor
Toronto, Ontario M5H 4E3, Canada
HanoverSqPress.com

Printed in U.S.A.

AUTHOR NOTE

Why do we dream?

A third of our lives is spent in sleep, yet as we dream we venture to wondrous and bizarre places. Are dreams merely subconscious illusions? Or are they something more profound?

Everyone has probably pondered these questions at one point or another. But I've clung to them as tightly as Linus clings to his blanket. The more we learn, the more insistent our curiosity becomes. And the more complicated our questions get, the more we wish for simple answers.

This is especially true for me when it comes to sleep and dreams. The unknown, mysterious rift between yesterday and today is a space I've found myself filling with joyful imagination. As I started writing this story, I enjoyed the way my imagination and reality fondly drew closer.

This is a story about a shopping village you can only enter when asleep. It's full of interesting people and places that capture the hearts of sleeping customers, like a food truck that sells snacks to ensure a good night's sleep, and the grumpy Noctilucas who frantically dress those customers who arrive without nightgowns. There's Maxim's back-alley nightmare-making workshop, as well as a mysterious dream maker hidden in a Million-Year Snow Mountain cabin. Products on offer range from Babynap Rockabye's conception dreams to the flying fantasies of Leprechauns.

But most of all, it is a collection of stories about the Dallergut Dream Department Store—the sleeping customers' favorite spot, so popular that once you try it, you'll always go back. Each floor offers unique dreams in special packaging, filling up the endless shelves and enhancing the customers' everyday lives. I hope this place holds a special place in your heart, too.

And lastly, if this story enriches your life at all and helps you have a good night's sleep—and a good night's dream—I could not be happier.

Miye Lee

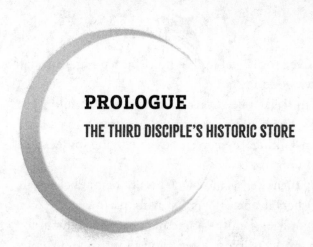

PROLOGUE
THE THIRD DISCIPLE'S HISTORIC STORE

Penny is sitting on the second floor of her favorite café. She's wearing a comfortable shirt. Her bobbed hair is soggy. This morning, she received word from the Dallergut Dream Department Store that her application has passed the screening, and her interview is next week. She went straight to a corner bookstore to buy job interview books, and now she is in full prep mode.

But something has been bothering her for a while. A guy drinking tea at the next table has been tapping his feet, showing off his colorful fuzzy socks with every bounce, distracting her like crazy.

He is in a thick dressing gown, sipping his tea with closed eyes. As he blows on his tea, its fresh forest scent carries over to her table. He must be having a special herbal tea good for fatigue.

"Hmm, very nice…warm…delicious… Should I get a refill?" The guy mutters under his breath as though he's sleep-talking, then goes back to tapping his feet and smacking his lips.

Penny turns her seat to block his bouncing socks from view. Others in the café are wearing pajamas.

For centuries, Penny's hometown has been famous for its sleep products. Now it has evolved into a metropolis with a surging population. The locals, including Penny, who grew up here, are used to seeing outsiders roaming around in sleepwear.

Penny sips on her now-cold coffee. The bitter caffeine seems to mute the background noise and cool the air around her. The extra charge for two Calm Syrup pumps is worth it. She pulls out her job prep questions and re-reads the last one, which she has been struggling with.

Q. Which dream and dreammaker won the Grand Prix at the 1999 Dream of the Year Awards by a unanimous vote?

    a. "Crossing the Pacific Ocean as a Killer Whale" by Kick Slumber

    b. "Living as My Parents for a Week" by Yasnoozz Otra

c. "Floating in Space Gazing Down on Earth" by
   Wawa Sleepland

d. "Teatime with a Historical Figure" by Doje

e. "An Infertile Couple's Dream Foretelling the Birth
   of Triplets" by Babynap Rockabye

Penny chews on her pen cap. The question is tricky: 1999 was a long time ago. Young dream directors like Kick Slumber or Wawa Sleepland might not be correct. She strikes out those two choices with her pen. When did Yasnoozz Otra's "Living as My Parents for a Week" come out? If Penny's memory serves, it was fairly recent. Otra's dreams usually receive heavy prerelease promotions, and a catchphrase from their ads is still vivid in her memory. "Still bothering to scold your kids? Make them live like you for a week in a dream, and everything is solved!"

Penny wavers between the two remaining options and finally goes with "e.," Babynap Rockabye's "An Infertile Couple's Dream Foretelling the Birth of Triplets." She reaches to take another sip of coffee when, out of nowhere, a furry paw slaps down on her question sheet, catching her so off guard that she nearly knocks over the mug.

"No, the answer is *a*," says the owner of the big paw without an introduction. "Kick Slumber debuted in 1999. He won the Grand Prix in his first year. I saved for six months straight to buy that dream. It was the most vivid dream I'd had in my entire life! The feeling of my fins crossing the ocean and the view under the waves. It was so real that when I woke up, I was devastated to remember that I wasn't a killer whale! He's a genius. You know how old he was then? Just thirteen!" The owner of the paw seems to burst with pride as if he were talking about his own accomplishment.

"Oh, it's you, Assam. You scared me." Penny pushes the mug out of harm's way. "How did you know I was here?"

"I saw you coming out of the bookstore with a bunch of books. I knew you'd come here. You never study at home." Assam glances at the pile of books on Penny's table. "Prepping for the job interview?"

"And how did you know *that*? I just heard from them this morning."

"Nothing in this area goes unnoticed by us Noctilucas."

Assam's job, like the other Noctilucas working on this street, is to make sure sleeping customers don't go around taking off their pajamas. They chase after any naked patrons with stacks of dressing gowns that hang from their oversize claws. That feature, combined with their warm, furry bodies, makes a good fit for the job. The irony is that they don't wear anything themselves, but on second thought, Penny thinks the naked customers would rather be chased by equally naked furry creatures than by well-dressed humans.

"You don't mind me sitting here, do you? My feet hurt from bustling around all day." Assam plops down next to Penny before she can answer. His fluffy tail sticks out through a hole in the back of the chair, wagging.

"This is hard." Penny looks at the question again. "How old are you if you know all this, Assam?"

"That's a rude question to ask a Noctiluca," Assam says primly. "I once studied hard to get into those stores too, but I quit. I thought this job suited me better." He slings a stack of gowns over his shoulder. "Anyhow, I can't believe this is really happening. Clumsy Penny, getting an interview at the Dallergut Dream Department Store!"

"I guess my good karma is finally catching up to me!" It's a miracle, Penny thinks, that she even passed the screening.

Everyone wants to work at the Dallergut Dream Department Store. The high pay, the glamorous architecture, the chance to work at a city landmark, the perks of free dreams doled out on special occasions. It's a sought-after job. Plus the locals are familiar with the long pedigree of the Dallergut family. In fact, the family *is* the origin of the city. The prospect of working with Mr. Dallergut makes Penny's heart so full that she thinks her whole body might swell up like a balloon.

"I really hope I can get in," Penny says, clasping her hands together as if in prayer.

"And you're studying just these materials?" Assam holds up one of the prep books and skims through it before putting it back on the table.

"Thought I should memorize whatever I can. You never know what they'll ask. I could have to name the Legendary Big Five, or the highest-selling dream of the decade, or what time of day is popular among what customer demographic—who knows? Apparently the shift I applied for has a lot of West Australian and Asian customers. I even memorized all the time zones and datelines. Fun fact, do you know why our city has a constant influx of customers twenty-four seven?"

Penny is eager to launch in, but Assam is equally eager to avoid her lecture, vigorously shaking his head. "Dallergut would never ask such a boring question. Plus any random middle schooler would know the answer."

When Penny turns glum, Assam holds out his paw to pat her on the shoulder. "Don't worry, friend. I've heard a lot about Dallergut after a decade of working here. And I hear he loves to ask open-ended questions about dreams, so I don't think his prompts will have a clear answer. Speaking of which, I actually came here to give you this." He drops the heap of dressing gowns from his shoulder and starts rummaging through them.

From the mountain of gowns, he produces a small bundle containing dozens of fuzzy socks.

"Wait, no, these are for the customers who have cold feet… Ah, yes, there it is!" Assam finds a small booklet among the socks. It has a hard, pale blue cover, and the elegant gold titling reads *The Time God and the Three Disciples*.

"I haven't seen that book in ages!" Penny recognizes the title at once. Everyone who grew up in her hometown had to read it.

"Dallergut could ask about this story, you know. If you haven't read it since you were little, you should read it again—carefully, this time." Assam pulls his seat closer, his face right next to Penny's. "And just between us, I hear Dallergut gave this book to all his employees at the Dream Department Store."

"For real?" Penny asks, clutching the book from Assam.

"Of course! That proves how important he thinks this boo—" Assam stops abruptly as his eyes move from Penny to the view outside the window. "Oh goodness! I should get back. I think I just saw a person roaming around in underwear." His chestnut nose twitches. He rushes to pick up the pile of gowns while Penny helps to put the fuzzy socks back in the bundle.

"Good luck, Penny. Let me know how the interview goes." Assam stands up, his eyes still preoccupied with the view outside. "At least he is wearing *something*," he mumbles.

"Thanks, Assam," Penny says.

Assam's tail circles clockwise as if to say, "You're welcome," and off he goes downstairs.

Penny inspects the book from Assam. He does have a point. *The Time God and the Three Disciples* explains the origin of this shopping street, the birth of the city, and most of all, the genesis of the Dallergut Dream Department Store. If Dallergut values history, there is a good chance that the answers to his interview questions will be in this book. Penny tucks the sheets of practice questions inside her backpack. She finishes her coffee in one gulp, straightens her back, then flips open the book.

THE TIME GOD
AND THE THREE DISCIPLES

Eons ago, there lived the Time God, who governed people's lives. One day during their usual relaxed luncheon, the Time God realized there was little time left. The Time God summoned three disciples and shared the news.

The First Disciple, gallant and daring, asked their teacher what they should do next. The vulnerable Second Disciple brimmed with tears, lost in the memories they shared with the Time God. The Third Disciple stood there without a word, waiting for the Time God to continue.

"My dearest Third Disciple, always considerate and cautious, let me ask you a question. If I divide time into three shards for each of you to govern, which shall you take—the past, the present or the future?" the Time God asked.

The Third Disciple pondered, then said they would choose whatever was left after the First and Second Disciples had chosen.

The gallant and daring First Disciple immediately made their selection. "Please grant me power not to dwell on the past so I can govern the future," they added.

The First Disciple always thought that having a fixed eye on the future was the most beautiful virtue. So, the Time God granted them the future with the power to forget the past.

The Second Disciple cautiously requested that they take the past. They said holding on to warm memories would make them happy forever. So, the Time God granted them the past with the power to forever cherish all old memories.

Now, holding the shard of the present—so small and sharp compared to the future and past—the Time God asked the Third Disciple, "Shall you govern the momentary present?"

"No, teacher, please distribute it to all people equally," the Third Disciple said.

The Time God was confused. "Throughout all my years of teaching, there was no particular time that you considered special?" the Time God asked in disappointment.

The Third Disciple's response was candid. "The time I love most is when everyone is asleep, teacher. In sleep we do not dwell on regrets about the past or anxiety over the future. We do not even recognize we are asleep in the present as it is happening. But I am a measly being, and could never request to govern such a time."

The First Disciple secretly scoffed at them, while the Second Disciple was mildly surprised. They both thought sleep was a waste of time. But the Time God generously offered sleep time to the Third Disciple.

"Dear First and Second Disciples, do you mind if I take slices from your shards, past sleep and future sleep, and give them to the Third Disciple?"

The First and Second Disciples answered without hesitation, "Not at all, teacher."

So, the three disciples took their portion of time shards and dispersed. The First and Second Disciples, who each received the future and past, were very satisfied with the powers given to them by the Time God.

The First Disciple and their followers let go of all the tedious things from the past and were soon excited to build a grand new future, venturing out to a land much bigger than their own. Equally excited were the Second Disciple and their followers, who cherished the past, remembering their young, fair-skinned faces and loving memories.

But problems soon arose. The First Disciple and their followers were so occupied with the future that the sheer amount of forgotten past started to stack like fog across their land. Through the dense layers of haze, they could no longer recognize their friends and family. As memories of their beloved kinfolk evaporated, so too did their sense of purpose, which had previously guided the future. They became oblivious to what lay right before them, and even more so of what lay ahead.

The Second Disciple and their followers were no different. They were trapped in only the good memories, so they could not accept the passage of time, the inevitable partings and deaths. Their tears constantly flowed across the earth, creating a large cave in which they eventually hid, burying themselves deep inside.

The Time God, having witnessed everything, waited until everyone was sound asleep. Then, beneath the moonlight, they snuck into their bedrooms. The Time God pulled out a sharp shard of the present and, with a hard grip, used it to slice off their shadows. Holding the shadows in one hand and an empty bottle in the other, the Time God left in the darkness.

First, the Time God put the foggy memories of the First Disciple and their followers in the bottle. Then, they filled it with all the tears of the Second Disciple and their followers. Lastly, the Time God went to the Third Disciple in secret.

"To what do I owe the pleasure of this unannounced visit at night, teacher?" the Third Disciple asked.

Without a word, the Time God pulled them out one by one and placed them on the table—the sleeping shadows, the bottle of forgotten memories and teardrops. The Third Disciple could not fathom what it all meant.

"How shall I help people with all this?" the Third Disciple asked, but instead of an answer, the Time God stuffed the saggy, deep-sleep shadows in the bottle. The shadows struggled to open their eyes.

Then a wonder occurred. The tears gathered to become the eyes of the shadows. The eyes opened wide, and the shadows came to life inside the bottle of memories.

"Let people's shadows be awake when they are asleep," said the Time God as they handed the bottle to the Third Disciple.

As wise as the Third Disciple was, they had no idea what their teacher meant. "Do you mean to let people think and feel, even in their sleep? How would that be any help for them?"

"The memories experienced during sleep will strengthen weak souls. And when they wake up the next day, they won't forget what's important."

After the Time God had delivered this speech, the Third Disciple realized their lesson was ending. They shouted in haste as their teacher faded little by little. "Please enlighten me further, teacher. How can I teach people to understand all this? I cannot even begin to define what *this* is."

The Time God smiled and said, "You do not need to understand. It is better that you do not. Time will come when people start to embrace it."

"Could you at least give this a name? Shall I call it a miracle? Or an illusion?" the Third Disciple asked desperately.

"Call it a dream. You will make them dream every night." And with that, the Time God vanished without a trace.

Penny closes the book, odd sensations stirring inside her. The story had seemed elusive and far-fetched when she first read it in childhood. A fairy tale. But the proof of its veracity solidified her understanding. The story is built into the fabric of the city, a part of the circle of life. The very fact that we dream every night is living proof. So is that fact that the Third Disciple went on to found the Dream Department Store, which passed through his descendants down to Dallergut.

Suddenly, Dallergut seems like a mythical figure to Penny. The thought of having a conversation with him one-on-one leaves her nervously excited. She shudders. *I guess I'm done studying for today*, she thinks.

Penny returns home, and for the rest of the day, until she falls asleep, she doesn't put down the book from Assam. She reads and rereads it over several days. She reads it so many times that she has memorized the entire story.

On the day of the interview, Penny arrives at the department store early, looking for Dallergut's office in the lobby on the first floor. People wear stretched T-shirts and loose shorts as pajamas, or dressing gowns rented by the Noctilucas. They are all looking at different dream products in the display corner. Next to the "Best New Products" stand, a customer in pajama bottoms covered with stars is holding a dream box. "Oh, the new dream by Kick Slumber is here… 'Becoming a Giant Tortoise in the Galapagos.' Let's see. These snobby critics even rated it four point nine out of five? That's rare. What's the description? 'A spectacular abyss surrounding its shell'? Their blurbs are confusing and useless as usual." Penny has ten minutes to get to Dallergut's office, but none of the spaces here look fancy enough to be his.

Penny intends to ask a middle-aged employee at the front desk, but she's on the phone and seems too busy. Same with the employees who hurry past in linen waist aprons, barely noticing Penny.

"Mom! I flunked it!" yells a passerby on the phone,

bumping into Penny. "He asked the craziest questions ever. I'd analyzed the last five years of dream trends, but he didn't ask anything about that!"

She must have had an interview with Dallergut! Desperately, Penny tries to silently mouth to her *Where. Is. The. Office?*

The woman bluntly points up the stairs before rushing through the crowd. A wooden staircase leads to the next floor. Looking closer, Penny spots a half-open wooden door with a dangling sign that reads Interview Room. The door's peeling paint and the rough handwriting on the sign make it look like the entrance to an old-school classroom.

In front of the door, Penny takes a moment to breathe and calm herself. Then, still unsure if this is Dallergut's office, she knocks.

"Yes, do come in." A booming voice rings from the inside. The same voice Penny has often heard in TV interviews or radio broadcasts. There is no doubt that Dallergut is inside the room.

"Excuse me."

The office is smaller than she expected. Dallergut is struggling with an old printer behind a long desk. "Welcome. Do you mind giving me a second? I have issues every time I print with this thing."

He is wearing a clean shirt, and looks taller and skinnier than he does on TV or in magazines. His disheveled, wavy hair shows streaks of gray. Dallergut forcibly pulls out what looks like Penny's résumé from the printer. Having been jammed somewhere inside the machine, the paper is crumpled and ripped, but he seems satisfied. "Finally."

Penny approaches and Dallergut offers his wrinkled, skinny hand. Penny, feeling nervous, wipes her hands on her shirt before shaking his. "Hello, Mr. Dallergut, I'm Penny."

"Nice to meet you, Penny. I was looking forward to meeting you." Dallergut looks regal. His dark brown eyes exude youthful twinkles, more like the eyes of a boy. Penny worries she's staring and looks away at the boxes strewn all over the office, which looks more like a shabby storeroom. All dream products. Some are damp from long days spent here, and some seem new with their wrapping still shiny. Dallergut pulls a steel chair closer, drawing Penny's attention back to him.

"Please have a seat." He points to a nearby chair. "Make yourself comfortable. These are my favorite cookies. Here, have some." Dallergut hands Penny a savory-looking nutty cookie.

"Thank you," Penny says, and as she takes a bite, the air turns cooler, and her shoulders relax. Strangely, the mysterious office becomes more familiar. The effect is similar to the Calm Syrup she adds to her coffee, only better. There must be something special in this cookie.

"I remember your name very clearly," Dallergut says. "Your application was impressive. I was struck by what you wrote. 'As much as you love them, dreams are just dreams.'"

"I'm sorry? Oh, that… That was…" She now remembers sprinkling the phrase into her otherwise bland application, hoping it might pique Dallergut's interest. *Did he just want to check who this daring kid was?*

Penny gauges Dallergut's expression. He seems genuinely interested in her.

"It is great to hear that I made an impression, sir," Penny carefully responds.

"Shall we get down to business, then?" Dallergut looks to the ceiling, gathering his thoughts. "First, I'd like to hear your honest opinion about dreams, Penny."

It's a tricky prompt to start with. Penny takes a deep breath and tries to remember the model answer she saw in the job interview prep books.

"So… Dreams let us experience things we otherwise couldn't in reality… They serve as a substitute to the unrealistic possibilities…" Penny notices Dallergut's disappointed glance and suspects that many interviewees who came before her would probably have answered in the same way.

"That doesn't sound like the person who wrote this application." Dallergut averts his gaze as he points to the crumpled document. Penny's gut tells her that responses like this will only lead to rejection. She needs to turn the tide.

"But even if we can experience the unrealistic in dreams, they can never be real." Penny has no idea what she's talking about. All she wants is to stand out from the rest of the applicants. She has a strong feeling this is what Dallergut is looking for above all. Plus, if the daring statement of "Dreams are just dreams" got her past the screening stage, she might as well stick to this path.

"No matter how good a dream you have, when you wake up, that is it."

"Why so?" Dallergut looks serious.

Penny is baffled. She has no idea how to build on her impromptu response. To buy time, she scarfs down the rest of the cookie, letting it soothe her. "No particular reason, sir. I just heard that customers mostly forget about their dreams afterward. I meant it literally, that dreams are just dreams, because they are gone once you wake up. And that's why they don't interfere with reality. I like how dreams don't overstep."

Penny swallows hard. She's rambling to fill the silence, worried it might ruin the interview. But now it's clear her answer has just killed the mood.

"I see. Is that all?" Dallergut asks indifferently.

The interview's over, she knows it. But Penny decides to take one more chance. She might as well mention her recent prep work.

"I've read *The Time God and the Three Disciples* many times. In the story, the Third Disciple rules sleep, which the other disciples overlooked."

Dallergut's expression shifts. She has his attention again. Perhaps Assam's suggestion had been spot-on.

"I didn't understand the Third Disciple's choice," Penny continues. "The First Disciple chooses the future, which has infinite possibilities. And the Second Disciple chooses the past, with all its precious experiences. Hopes for the future and lessons from the past. These two are very important elements of living in the present."

Dallergut nods subtly. Penny doesn't stop.

"But what about when we're asleep? Nothing happens. We just lie down for hours. Nominally we're resting, but some people think it's a waste of time. Because if you think about it, dozens of years of your life are spent just lying down! Yet the Time God leaves sleep to their most beloved Third Disciple and asks them to make people dream during sleep. Why is that?" Penny lets the question hang in the air for a moment, buying herself some time. "Whenever I think of dreams, I ask myself this question, what do people seek in sleep? I think we're all insecure and foolish in our own way. Some of us are like the First Disciple, always looking ahead. Others linger in the past like the Second Disciple. But for all of us, it's easy to forget what's important. I think the Time God assigns sleep time to the Third Disciple to help people. You know how yesterday's worries are gone after a good night's sleep, and we are fully refreshed to start a new day? That's it! Whether you experience a good dream purchased from this department store or don't dream at all, we all sleep to get closure on yesterday and prepare for tomorrow. In that sense, sleep is no longer a waste of time."

Inspired by Assam's book, Penny has managed to come up with a decent answer. She's surprised by her own eloquence. *Reading books does go a long way, as they say.* Confidence restored, she wants to end with a flourish.

"So I think sleep and dreams are…like a comma God meticulously designed in the middle of a breathless sentence called life!" she concludes proudly. Dallergut looks inscrutable. Penny's lips tighten. Her last sentence was too on the nose. She should have stopped when things were going great.

Silence hangs in the air. Dallergut's office feels a world apart from the crowds of customers shopping downstairs. Penny suddenly feels parched. Dallergut scribbles something on her résumé.

"Thank you for your insights. You seem to have given

a lot of thought to dreams." Dallergut clasps his hands and looks straight into her eyes. "Let me end with my last question. As you know, there are many other dream stores besides ours. Please tell me why you want to join us in particular."

Penny's instinct is to mention the high pay, but that would be too blunt. She chooses her words carefully. "Dream stores are springing up everywhere and selling provocative dreams. I remember something you said in the magazine *More Interpretations Than Dreams*. You mentioned that some stores lure people in by offering excess sleep, purely for pleasure, more sleep than anyone would need. I've heard that your store is different. You only offer dreams that underscore the importance of reality. I think these were the boundaries the Time God wanted the Third Disciple to govern. Just the right amount of control without overstepping. That's why I applied here."

Dallergut finally gives a wide smile, which Penny thinks makes him look a decade younger. His dark brown eyes gaze steadily at her.

"Penny, can you start tomorrow?"

"Of course!" Suddenly the noises behind the door start seeping into the office room again. Penny officially has a job.

ONE

THE DALLERGUT DEPARTMENT STORE RUSH HOUR

It is Penny's first day of work, and she's already running late, gasping and panting, with beads of sweat on the bridge of her nose. She had a celebratory dinner with her family yesterday before chatting the night away with her friends, hence the oversleeping. The call with Assam went on for an especially long time as he was very keen to know all the ways in which his book had been helpful.

"So when you said that, how did his face change again? Oh, my goodness, that book was indeed the silver bullet! You know, the book *I* gave you, right?"

Penny promised to treat him to a nice meal in return, finally getting him to hang up the phone.

Today, the city is especially busy with locals and out-of-town sleep customers. Penny quickly pushes through the crowd, knocking shoulders and apologizing. She finally catches her breath when she arrives at the back alley of the Dallergut Department Store. She might just make it on time.

The alley is filled with the savory scents of roasted fruits and boiling milk. Having skipped breakfast, she looks around to see if she can pick up a fruit skewer, but the line is too long.

"What's up with today? So many people," says a flustered food-truck cook. He's flipping over fruit skewers on the grill with one hand and ladling a massive pot with the other. Caramelized onion milk is boiling inside the pot. It's a popular recipe, known for inducing deep sleep.

Several customers are already sipping onion milk from mugs in front of the food truck. The elder customers look relaxed and satisfied, but the kids take sips and scowl. One deliberately spills milk on the floor.

"No waste on the floor, please!" A Noctiluca appears out of nowhere, shaking his furry paws as he steps in between the kids and Penny. Smaller than Assam, he starts wiping the milk from the floor, grumbling. Penny quickly moves away so as not to get any milk on her socks. She's not wearing shoes today as she wanted to run fast and comfortably.

In fact, it is not uncommon to walk around without shoes here. The street's strict sanitation policy ensures it's as clean as an indoor floor, so sleeping customers can kick off their shoes. Naturally, the locals have also taken to walking in socks for a quick stroll.

But this has caused an unexpected crisis for the Leprechauns, who have been artisan shoemakers for generations. People now shop more for socks and less for shoes, which has hurt the shoe business. As a result, the Leprechauns have expanded their business ventures into the dream-production sector. Assam told Penny that their revenues soared by 1,000 percent after their expansion. That sounds believable, given that the Leprechauns' shoe store has just moved from a cheap corner spot to a bigger space in the main street.

As she passes, Penny glances at the Leprechauns' store window display, located right next to the Dallergut Dream Department Store. It has a big sign and lots of other product posters here and there, making it hard to see the inside of the store.

LOOKING FOR WINGED SHOES, LIGHTSPEED SKATE SHOES, AND SPECIAL FLIPPERS FOR GRACEFUL SWIMMING? COME INSIDE! INTERESTED IN A FLYING DREAM, SPRINTING DREAM, OR SWIMMING DREAM THAT HARNESSES THE ESSENCE OF THE LEPRECHAUNS' MASTER TECHNOLOGY? VISIT US IN THE DALLERGUT DREAM DEPARTMENT STORE NEXT DOOR, ON THE THIRD FLOOR!

"Papa, can I have winged shoes?" a girl asks her dad.

"Those shoes break easily, sweetie. The best shoes don't have fancy features, just strong soles."

"I'm not leaving until you buy me those shoes!" She flops down, throwing a temper tantrum.

Penny passes the father and daughter and finally arrives at the Dream Department Store. She pulls out a pair of loafers from her purse and does a last-minute check of her reflection in a compact mirror. Her bobbed hair looks elegant today. With her cute nose and big, gentle eyes, she should make a good first impression. The only downside is the wrinkled blouse she forgot to iron, but she can do nothing about it now.

As she steps inside the department store, she is greeted by an enormous throng of customers. At the lobby's front desk, an employee is making announcements into a microphone. It is the same middle-aged woman Penny saw yesterday, who was busy on the phone.

"Attention, new out-of-town customers. All costs are deferred! You may leave once you receive your dream! Hey, Dojicom siblings! That doesn't apply to you. You guys come and pay first!" A young, freckled brother and sister get caught trying to sneak through the back door. They trudge toward the front desk.

Penny is confused about whether she should go to Dallergut's office first or just change into her employee apron. In her waffling, someone yanks her by the hem and pulls her behind the front desk.

"You're new today, right? Nice to meet you. Now stay on your toes. We have a busy day today." The middle-aged woman who was just giving announcements smiles at Penny. "My name is Weather," she continues. "I'm the first-floor manager. But forget the title, just call me Weather. I have a daughter around your age and a baby boy. Been working here for thirty years. That's pretty much all you need to know about me."

She seems bright and cool but looks exhausted. Her red curly hair is drooping, and her voice has gone raspy.

"Hi, Weather. I'm Penny. And you're right. Today's my first day. And so… What should I do first?"

"Dallergut asked me to give you a tour. As you know, each of our five floors sells different genres of dreams. You don't need to worry about the first floor—Dallergut and myself, with other veteran employees, handle the customers here. From the second to the fifth floor, you'll go upstairs and meet each floor manager. They'll explain their floors to you. Then, you can tell us which floor you want to work on. But if none of the managers like you, well, you may have to go home…"

Penny blinks her large eyes in shock.

"I was just joking." Weather shakes her hand. She looks hot, and as she takes off her jacket, her shirt is drenched with sweat, even with the air-conditioning. "Now, off you go. I gotta get back to work. So many customers today."

Penny departs, and Weather quickly disappears behind a flock of customers pushing toward the front desk. She can hear her yelling, "What about 'The Reunion with an Old Friend' product? There's only one left in stock on the second floor! Were you asking what kind of old friend it would be? I have no idea! Possibly a childhood friend that you still remember?"

"'Three Nights in the Maldives' was out of stock as soon as they came in."

"I'm sorry, but this dream is already reserved. No ripping the package!"

"Chuck Dale's 'Five Senses of Sensual Dream Series' was just taken a minute ago by a group of teenage customers."

"All floors will be sold out soon. ALL DREAMS WILL BE SOLD OUT SOON!"

Away from Weather's desperate calls, Penny turns toward the elevator. There's already a long line forming, so she decides to take the staircase next to Dallergut's office. She wonders if she should stop by and say hello, but after seeing a handwritten sign that reads Temporarily Away she decides to return later. Dallergut's printer must still be broken. The wooden staircases are so steep that by the time Penny reaches the second floor, her thighs already feel numb. At least she won't need additional workouts.

At first glance, the second floor looks clean, without a speck of dust. A simple wooden interior and evenly placed lighting fixtures. Even the product tags look as consistent as clockwork. Most of the display stands are empty, but the few items still in stock are placed at exactly the same angle, each with the same ribbon tied to them. The employees in their aprons walk around the display stands, conscientious and anxious as they look after the prospective buyers, who inspect various products and put them back in a disorderly fashion.

While the first floor sells only a handful of high-end, popular or limited-edition, preordered products, the second floor sells more generic dreams. Also known as "The Daily" corner, the second floor displays dreams of simplicity. Dreams of quick getaways, hanging out with friends, and enjoying good food.

In front of the staircase where Penny stands is a display case marked Memories. Inside it is a luxurious leather case labeled No Refund Once Unsealed. Only a few dreams remain.

"What is this dream about?" a woman calls after examining a product.

"It replays a favorite childhood memory in your dream! The stories differ depending on the dreamer. In my case, I had a dream where I lay on my mother's lap while she cleaned my ears. Her scent and the languid atmosphere—it was all so real. It was wonderful." The employee stares into space, daydreaming.

"I'll have it, then. Can I buy a few?"

"Of course. Lots of customers buy two or three a night."

Penny stands on her tiptoes to get a better look at the second floor. A middle-aged man who seems to be the floor manager is talking to a customer in a corner that has been decorated like a modern bedroom. Penny carefully approaches him so as not to interrupt their conversation.

His look really does scream "Manager." While all other employees wear aprons and a brooch carved with the number "2," he flaunts a lavish jacket, the brooch on his left lapel. He seems wiry and shrewd.

"Why can't I buy it?" asks a young male customer, confused.

"I'm sorry, but how about you come by another time? I'm afraid you're too distracted right now, which only obscures the clarity of the dream. It's better to have a good night's sleep first. I've seen countless customers like yourself whose thoughts creep in and alter their dreams entirely. There's some amazing onion milk on the next street. It helps with sleep. I'd recommend that you come back when you're well-rested."

The customer grumbles and goes off toward the elevator. The man who looks like the manager picks up the product the customer left behind, wipes it with his handkerchief, and places it back on the shelf, carefully straightening the angle.

"Excuse me… Are you the manager for the second floor?" Penny asks cautiously. He's wearing pristinely ironed trousers, his shoes are spotless, and his mustache is neatly trimmed. His cropped hair is pulled back with oily wax. Penny finds him intimidating.

"Yes, I am. Vigo Myers is my name. First day of work here?"

"Er, yes. I'm Penny. How did you know?" Penny covers her cheeks to hide any indication of "amateur" or "newbie" on her face.

"Customers rarely come to me first. They usually call for other employees. They say I'm not easy to talk to, which I don't mind. So that gave you away, and you didn't look familiar. It was a natural deduction." Myers folds his arms and gives Penny a stern look. "You must be on a floor tour. I remember the boss mentioning you."

"Yes, that's right."

"Good. Any questions about my floor?"

Penny's biggest question is how they can tie all those

ribbons into such perfect bows atop every single product, but she asks her second-biggest question instead.

"Why didn't you sell the dream to that customer?"

"Good question." Myers stretches his arms and strokes one of the display stands. "I've meticulously inspected and curated all the dreams on this floor. They're some of the store's best products. The last thing I want is for a customer to come back complaining that the dream didn't live up to expectations. Remember—you shouldn't sell dreams to just anybody, or you won't get the compensation each dream deserves."

Penny knows the store takes deferred payments from out-of-town customers, but that's all she knows. She nods, pretending she understands, but Myers senses otherwise.

"Newbies these days. I heard all they do is bring a cover letter and have a quick interview with Dallergut. And just like that, they're in!" Myers scoffs sotto voce.

"Yes... I mean, that's how I got in, too."

"Well, that's preposterous! I'm thinking of requiring another round of tests for the employees on my floor. The instability of dreams, and their malleable and perilous nature, cannot be grasped with moderate knowledge. No, sir! Did you know I double-majored in Dreamatography and Dream Neuroscience? My thesis was published in more academic journals than I can count. My knowledge has been enormously helpful in my work here. Weather may have gotten her manager position on the first floor because she's worked with Dallergut longer, but I've earned my place purely by talent. You don't think I'm here by luck, do you?"

"Of course not. That's amazing!"

Penny doesn't want to take extra tests just to work on the second floor. It seems that Myers realizes this, as he steps back to shout at his employees. "All right, everyone! All remaining items on the third display be consolidated to the first! Let's move. Chop-chop!"

"Yes, manager!"

The employees activate at Myers's command. Their smooth linen aprons make Penny keenly aware of the wrinkled edges of her blouse, which she struggles to pull straight as she heads upstairs.

The third floor is merrier by comparison. The product posters adorning the wall are artfully arranged, forming a colorful, eye-catching wallpaper. A recent hit song plays through the speakers.

The excitement among dream buyers, not to mention the employees, is palpable. One staffer is in full sales mode with a customer, intent on selling a fancy dream box with powder-pink, heart-shaped ornaments dangling from it.

"Chuck Dale's Sensual Dream Series is always out

of stock. How about this one by Keith Gruer? If you're lucky enough, you might go on a dream date with your dream date in your dream!" As the customer nods with interest, the employee adds, almost inaudibly, "The caveat is that depending on your condition, the person you go on a date with may be completely random."

The third-floor staff seem more carefree. All seem to have modified their work aprons to their own liking. One has hers turned into a princess-style dress, another has a badge with a picture of his favorite dreammaker. One staffer, busy replacing a small bulb inside a display case, has a huge pocket sewn onto her apron, filled with a stash of chocolate bars.

Penny looks around for someone who resembles a manager, but no one seems to stand out. She approaches a nearby employee cleaning a display case, wearing a typical linen apron.

"Excuse me, can you direct me to the floor manager? Today's my first day and I'm on a floor tour."

"Oh my God—a newbie! You're looking at her. Mogberry here. I'm the manager on the third floor."

She's wearing the same uniform as the other employees. Her short, curly hair is tied back, but thin baby hairs stick out all over. Mogberry looks too young to be a manager, her rosy cheeks adding to her youthful appearance.

Penny gives her a polite bow. "My name is Penny.

Dallergut instructed me to take a look around the store, so here I am."

"So I've heard. Welcome to the third floor!" says Mogberry with a wide smile. "This is where all the groundbreaking activity-based dreams are. Oh, sorry, would you excuse me for a second?" Mogberry turns to a hovering customer. "Can I help you, mister? Any specific dream you're looking for? If you have a preference, let me know. I can offer some recommendations."

The customer is wearing sporty shorts and a sleeveless top with a deep, plunging neckline. He looks young. Perhaps he's a middle schooler. He keeps rubbing his hands together.

"I'm looking for one where I'm the center of attention. Better if the whole world revolves around me. The last dream I bought, I showed off a cool rap performance in front of the entire class at a school festival, and I felt like one of the popular kids."

"There aren't many left in stock… Oh, how about a dream related to this sci-fi movie series? Superhero movies are big these days. You can be like Iron Man or the Incredible Hulk. The dreammaker, Celine Gluck, is famous for her attention to detail. It would be totally immersive."

"Awesome. I love superhero movies! In fact, I just saw one at the theater today! So yes, I'll definitely have one, please!"

Mogberry smiles in satisfaction. The customer tucks the product under his arm and moves to the other side of the floor to keep browsing.

Penny suddenly remembers the notice she saw hanging in the Leprechauns' shoe store window on her way to work.

"I heard 'Flying Dream' by the Leprechauns is on the third floor. Are those sold out?" she asks.

Mogberry, who has been all smiles, suddenly frowns. "Flying dreams are always out of stock. Do you know how cunning these Leprechaun scoundrels are? I wouldn't say I liked it from the beginning when those shoe-making brats started getting into the dream business out of the blue. Sure enough, I caught them sneaking in dreams that make you feel immobile, like your feet are made of steel! They say it's good for business. That those dreams pay more. When I called them out on it, they threatened to stop supplying us. Only they can make those types of dreams. I mean, what nonsense is that?"

Penny regrets not having studied the dream payment system. Why do those immobile dreams pay better? She can't understand the logic. She knows of books like *The Economics of Deferred Dream Payments* and *Sell Dreams, Buy a House*, but she has never dared to read them. She is hopeless with money or anything number-related for that matter. Penny wants to ask Mogberry but decides not to.

She's afraid of coming across as underqualified and jeopardizing her chances of getting a job on any of the floors.

"Dallergut is too much of a softie. I think he should cut a deal with the Leprechauns!" the third-floor manager grumbles. As she grows more disgruntled, the curly baby hairs on the crown of her head spring out like mini Slinkies, spraying loose from her ponytail.

Penny starts to peek around, looking for a way out to the fourth floor as Mogberry's complaining drags on and on. Thankfully, another employee passes by and Mogberry finds a fresh audience for her grumbling about the Leprechauns. Penny slips away.

Secretly, she has high hopes for the fourth floor. It sells nap-exclusive dreams, and she hears these are popular among animal customers, who tend to sleep lightly, or baby customers, who struggle with nap time. Basically, she would be surrounded by adorable customers while working, and that alone is enough reason to build anticipation.

When Penny reaches the fourth floor, she spots a few adorable tiny customers, but overall, it is not quite as she imagined it. There are lots of adults and scary-looking animals here, too. The fourth floor's ceiling is lower than the others. The displays only reach as far as her ankles. She feels like she's at a flea market where products are strewn across large mats.

Sticking close to the wall, Penny tries to sidestep a

sloth lying in the middle of the corridor while a giggling toddler pokes it. By Penny's feet, a display reads, "Playing with Owner." An old, furless dog sniffs around to carefully select a dream. Penny steps aside, careful not to disturb the canine customer.

"Knock, knock." Someone taps on Penny's back, startling her. She turns around to find a man in a jumpsuit with long, disheveled hair, staring at her.

"Hiya, you must be the newbie. Why didn't you come see me first, dear?" he asks slyly.

"Oh, hello. I'm Penny. I got carried away, just looking around… Are you the manager of the fourth floor?"

"Sure am! I'm Speedo, and I'm the manager, indeed! Who else would it be?" Speedo is a fast talker. "This floor is always busy. There's just so much demand. D'you know what the most important thing is on this floor?"

Penny has no clue, but Speedo seems determined to carry on. He runs a hand through his long hair and raises his chin with its chicken scratch goatee. Penny focuses on the silver brooch on his chest, carved with the number "4."

"Of course you don't know. Listen carefully. The key is to make sure these napping customers don't sleep too deeply from our dreams. Long naps make babies cry, and deep slumber makes animals easy prey. So, when in doubt, it's best not to sell our dreams at all. The other floors will generate the biggest sales, anyway."

Speedo doesn't stop showing off. He must have been dying to do so, with so few people around to boast to.

"Any questions for me?"

"Well—" Penny tries to come up with something, but Speedo cuts her off.

"You wanted to ask why I'm wearing this jumpsuit, didn't you? People always ask me that!"

Penny fails to hide her "Well, no" expression, but fortunately, Speedo doesn't care.

"I've always felt that putting on a shirt and pants separately is a waste of time. I would rather get more sleep in the morning. Oh, you must wonder—how do I go to the bathroom with this on? Clothes nowadays are so cleverly designed; you unzip it here—"

"Thanks, Speedo, but no need. I think I get it."

"Well then. Mind getting out of my way? Pretty soon the nappers from Spain will start flocking in." Speedo takes off as hastily as he's been talking. In an instant, he's already conversing with customers. "Oh, you have a good eye! The one you're looking at is called 'Fatigue Recovery.' Only two left in stock. There's no better nap dream than this! What do you think? Would you like one or two?"

Startled, the customer puts down the product and trots

off. Now more of them are leaving, overwhelmed by Speedo's aggressive customer service, but Speedo seems oblivious as he continues to sweep across the floor.

"Hey, Penny, you still here?" Speedo calls out, then before she knows it, he's hovering right by her.

Penny hopes she won't be assigned to the fourth floor. But she's also feeling increasingly distraught. There is still the fifth floor, but the fifth floor only sells leftover dreams from the other four floors. She can't imagine that the fifth floor will offer a better work environment.

The first thing she notices when she arrives on the fifth floor are the chaotic banners everywhere. She pushes one aside, which reads Blowout Sale on Expiring Products!

The fifth floor is much more crowded than the other floors, filled with customers and employees. A slew of dream boxes on the central display looks like they've been unceremoniously dumped there. Sticky notes and signs are sloppily plastered across the stand.

80% OFF SUPER SALE!
PLEASE NOTE:
ALL DREAMS HERE ARE IN BLACK AND WHITE.
IF YOU WISH TO PURCHASE COLOR VERSIONS,
PLEASE REACH OUT TO STAFF ON OTHER FLOORS.

Below the signs lie dream boxes with hashtags like: #EatingAWholeLobsterAtAPrivateBeach and #Sunset-OnTheSouthernIslandShore. Penny pictures a black-and-white scene—a black lobster and the somber gray ocean—then shakes her head. *So this is what you call a buy cheap, buy twice situation*, she thinks.

"Dear customers, this is a real treasure hunt! Some dreams were originally priced at fifty gordens, and you can also find dreams made by the Legendary Big Five! Some are limited editions! They are all hiding in here somewhere, waiting to be found! Keep your eyes peeled for your very own treasures!"

An employee is standing on one of the displays, gesturing wildly, his back to Penny. Round shoulders, a chubby build, nimble movements... His silhouette seems strangely familiar.

"Motail!"

"Penny! Are *you* the new hire? I had no idea!" Motail excitedly crouches down and greets her warmly. Penny's high-school friend and one of the loudest students, he always loved to be the center of attention. He did great impersonations of their teachers, too.

"Are you the manager here...?"

"Of course not! Though I hope so one day. There is no manager on the fifth floor. We can sell dreams however we want. Perfect for me!" As Motail talks, his body keeps bouncing around, and he continues point-ing out dreams to the customers below him. "Today's on me, guys! You can buy one, get one free! Out of my own salary!"

"Are you sure you can make a call like that?" Penny asks worriedly.

"It's a lie. I was selling it at double the price in the first place." Motail takes off his corduroy jacket and drapes it over his shoulders as he continues to hawk products. This place does suit him perfectly. But when Penny tries to picture herself dancing around and selling dreams on the display like Motail, her heart sinks.

"Hey, Penny! Look at these. Some great products just came in!"

Motail jumps down from the display and hands her a dream box with a translucent blueish wrapper.

"Is this…?"

"Yes! It's by Wawa Sleepland. 'A Week in Tibet'! The view will be gorgeous. Of course, bits and pieces will be in black-and-white, but still. I'm sure you know that Sleepland creates scenery that's even more awesome than what you might find in real life."

"But how come such a precious dream ended up here?" Penny is confused. Wawa Sleepland is one of the Legendary Big Five. Her dreams have months-long wait lists and are rarely available.

"One of her customers ordered a custom dream but failed to pick it up in time. I heard the dreamer was a student, and it was during midterms or something, and they apparently pulled an all-nighter and couldn't use it. Any products not picked up in time also end up here on the fifth floor. I'm going to hide this until my shift ends, then I'll take it with me," says Motail, smiling mischievously as he pushes the box deep inside the space below the display stand. "Please don't say anything to Dallergut, Penny! I want to keep my job," he adds, showing his snaggletooth grin. "And also, give some thought to applying to the fifth floor. You get incentives for your sales on our floor!"

Penny's eyes grow wide.

Motail adds, "But the base wage is way low."

It's time for Penny to return to the first floor to meet Dallergut. Instead of taking the elevator, she takes the stairs to give herself some time to think.

She weighs the risks of working on each floor. If she chooses the fifth floor, she'd have to train herself to be an extrovert. In other words, she'd need to become a new person. The fourth floor would require her work with Speedo. The third floor seems fun enough, except she'd need to be careful about what topics she discusses with Mogberry. And to work with Vigo Myers on the second floor, well, she'd need to start ironing her blouse every day before she even tries to pass his test. Just as she passes the second floor, she hears Myers shouting, "All products are sold out on the second floor! All sold out!"

Penny arrives on the first floor in front of Dallergut's office, still undecided about where she wants to work. The Temporarily Away sign is now gone, and the door is ajar. She peeks inside. Dallergut has company—it's Weather from the front desk.

"Dallergut, we are too old and worn out. We're long past the days when a cheap lunch box was all we needed to recharge, and that was thirty years ago. We need more people at the front desk. It's too much work for the two of us to handle. Just look at us today. You were unavailable all day, taking care of the preorders in your office and keeping track of the inventories. I almost passed out covering for you," Weather complains.

"I'm sorry, Weather. But you know how important the front desk job is. I can't entrust it to anyone. I'll try to post an opening internally to see if anyone within our staff is interested. Can you hang in there a little longer? The work can get overwhelming, so I'm not quite sure if anyone's up for it... Maybe Vigo Myers from the second floor?"

"Myers?" Weather asks.

"With his experience and knowledge, he should be a great help," Dallergut says gently.

"Oh, I don't think he would like the idea of working *for* me. Unless we offer him a managerial position for the first floor... Wait, who's there?" Weather senses Penny's presence and turns toward the door.

Penny tries to remain calm as she walks in. "I'm sorry, I didn't mean to interrupt. I just wanted to stop by and say I finished touring all the floors..."

"Oh, I see. Come in! Please have a seat." Dallergut greets Penny with delight. He's wearing a soft cardigan, leaning back in his chair. "So, which floor do you want to apply for?" he asks.

"If I were you, I would choose the second floor. I can't say Vigo Myers is easy to work with, but you'll learn a lot from him," Weather adds. She also seems interested in hearing Penny's answer.

But Penny now knows that an appealing position has just opened up. And she doesn't want to let that opportunity slip away.

After a pause, she says in a firm voice, "I want to work at the front desk."

To her surprise, Dallergut and Weather accept her proposal without hesitation. Weather seems especially delighted to have the extra support right away. And Dallergut, who must have been afraid that Weather might quit, seems relieved that Penny has swooped in and saved him.

The three walk out to the front desk so that Penny can be briefed on her new job. Behind them multiple security monitors follow the state of each floor. Next to the microphone sits a pile of brochures for customers.

"Here, you can track each floor's inventory, sales and dream payment statuses," Weather says, as she pulls up several complex windows on the computer monitor. "This is Dream Pay Systems Version 4.5. It's the ultimate all-inclusive software with everything you need to run a store. The dream payment balance feature is top-notch. Comes with a steep cost, but it's all worth it. And if you want to use the automatic balance system that links to the safe... When the inventory falls below fourteen percent, it'll trigger an automatic warning..."

Penny is trying to stay focused, but she's struggling to pay attention to Weather's tutorial. Surprisingly, Dallergut is wearing the same vacant look.

"I see you're another Dallergut, just as tech-averse. I'll tell you what the Eyelid Scale is."

"Now *that's* something I can weigh in on!" Dallergut brightens.

A towering wall of fully packed shelves curves behind the front desk. On each shelf sits a series of numbered scales, their pendulums swinging up and down like eyelids, indicating sleep status. At eye level, Penny spots a scale labeled No. 902, its marker quickly moving up and down between "awake" and "sleepy."

"These are for our regulars. Specifically designed to predict their visiting hours. A feature specific to our store," Dallergut says with a proud look.

"This customer's eyelids used to get droopy around now," Weather says, looking sentimentally at Eyelid Scale No. 999. "But as he aged, he started sleeping less. He rarely comes to buy dreams nowadays. You see, I have a fond affection for many of our customers. When a regular forgets to pick up a preorder in time, I'll stroke their eyelids to help get them to sleep. But you should refrain from that, really; you never know if they're in the middle of something important where they can't afford to doze off."

Penny is so busy writing down notes that she barely has time to answer. "Sorry, can you repeat what you just said? You do what to the eyelids?"

"It's fine. No worries—I'll be working next to you anyway."

The three are engrossed in this Eyelid Scale discussion when an alarm goes off. It's coming from the Dream Pay Systems monitor that Weather so highly praises.

Ding Dong. "ALL PRODUCTS SOLD OUT. WE ARE CLEARED OF ALL STOCK!"

"Work's done for today now that everything's sold

out," Dallergut says as he checks the notification and then announces through the microphone that everyone can leave work early. A cheer echoes across the store.

"It's been ages since this happened! I should leave early, too. I have a family gathering tonight. My youngest can finally do a handstand! So we're going to celebrate," Weather laughs.

All the employees, including Weather, leave one by one, until only Dallergut and Penny are left. Penny also wants to leave, but she's waiting for her boss to go first, and he's still in the office. Outside, a few stray customers linger around the front gate.

"I'm sorry, all our products are sold out. We'll reopen tomorrow as soon as we restock."

Penny tries to feign her best apologetic look. A handful of customers in their sleepwear shrug and turn to leave.

Dallergut, meanwhile, is scribbling something on a piece of paper at the front desk.

"What are you writing?" Penny asks.

"A sold-out notice to hang on the front gate."

Penny stands quietly, watching Dallergut. He has already thrown away three sheets of paper and is on the fourth because, apparently, he doesn't like his handwriting. Penny still finds it surreal that she's working with Dallergut, let alone standing right next to him.

"Is the Third Disciple from the story really one of your ancestors?" Penny asks, surprised by her own boldness.

"That's what I'm told. My parents and grandparents always reminded me of that," Dallergut responds nonchalantly as he picks bits of fluff from his cardigan.

"That's amazing." Penny looks at Dallergut in awe.

"Done!" he exclaims, finally finishing off the sign.

"Here, let me put it up for you." Penny takes out two long lines of tape and sticks the notice nice and firmly. She stands back to check that it is straight before she comes back in.

ALL PRODUCTS ARE SOLD OUT TODAY!
THANK YOU TO OUR CUSTOMERS FOR VISITING
THE DALLERGUT DREAM DEPARTMENT STORE ON YOUR WAY TO SLEEP.
PLEASE COME BACK TOMORROW!
WE ARE OPEN ALL YEAR-ROUND, TWENTY-FOUR SEVEN.
WE'LL ALWAYS HAVE FANTASTIC DREAM PRODUCTS WAITING FOR YOU.

YOURS TRULY,
DALLERGUT

"Time for some snacks!" Dallergut hums as he opens a packet labeled Calm Cookies, the same ones he offered Penny at her interview. "Wait, why are you still here, Penny? You should go home."

"Well… I was just… Since you're still here…"

"Oh, no. I'm kind of already off," Dallergut says, ambiguously.

"Pardon?"

"I actually live in the attic of this building. It's been remodeled for my use."

"Oh…"

Jingle.

The doorbell rings, and in comes an elderly customer.

"I'm sorry, we're out of stock today," says Penny, but Dallergut steps in, signaling for Penny to wait as he walks forward.

"Actually, I'm not here to buy anything. Do you take preorders?" the customer asks.

"Of course, please come over here." Dallergut deftly hides the cookie behind his back and welcomes the customer in, followed by a couple more. They're different ages and genders, but their eyes are all swollen. They must have cried before going to sleep.

"Something must've happened to them," Penny whispers to Dallergut.

"Looks like it. I know them all. They're actually here later than usual."

"They must've tossed and turned before falling asleep."

"Quite possibly."

Dallergut takes them to the staff lounge near the

entrance. Penny follows, and Dallergut doesn't seem to mind.

They pass through a creaky arched door into an expansive room with a chandelier that gives off a warm, cozy glow. There are ragged floor cushions, a couch and a long wooden table. An old fridge, a coffee machine and snack basket in the kitchen.

The customers sit and Dallergut doles out candies from the snack basket. "This is called Deep Sleep Candy. Sweet and effective. Perfect for sleepless nights like tonight."

As they take the candies, some of the customers begin to cry.

"I'm sorry, I should've given you Calm Cookies first," says Dallergut. "But no worries. You can cry all you want. Whatever happens here stays here. Now, what dream shall I prepare for you?"

"I broke up with my partner a few days ago." A young woman sitting by the entrance opens up first. "I've been okay, coping with it well, but today I had a sudden migraine, and my heart began to ache like crazy. I don't feel lonely, but just miserable. Ever since the breakup, I can't seem to move on, not even one step. I can't tell if what I'm feeling is regret or resentment. Will I understand if I see him again in my dream?"

"I lost my older sister when I was little. We had a big

age gap. And yesterday was my twenty-fifth birthday. The same age my sister was when she passed away. It dawns on me just how young she was when she left, and it hurts so much. I would love to see her, at least in my dreams, and have a chat. Do you think she's doing okay?"

"The contest deadline is coming up soon, but I still have no idea what to submit. Everyone else seems to have brilliant, sparkling ideas, and I feel so dumb. I'm getting old, I don't have any other skills, and I can't seem to give up on my dream."

"I turned seventy last month. It's been a long, full life. I was packing to move into a new home today and came across some pictures of myself from my student days, and of my wedding. And those old memories have been haunting me all day. Then, as I lay in bed, sorrow crept over me. The way time has flown by felt so cruel."

The customers all have their own stories to tell, and it takes a long while, as Dallergut takes thorough notes. "Thank you, everyone," he says eventually. "Your pre-order applications are all filled out. We'll start preparing your dreams."

The customers finish the Deep Sleep Candy and stand to leave.

"When can we expect to receive our dreams?" asks the old lady, who is the last one to stand up.

"Let me see… For some of you, I can get them right away, but the rest of you may have to wait a bit longer."

"How long?"

"I can't say with certainty, but there's one thing you all need to do to receive your dreams intact."

"What is it?"

"You must try to get a deep sleep every night. That's all."

The customers finally leave the store. Standing next to Dallergut, who is busy compiling all the notes, Penny gets ready to take off.

"Do you take these kinds of made-to-order dreams often?" she asks.

"Not too often. But sometimes. I always find it more rewarding than selling premade dreams. You'll understand one day when you run a store like me. Now, off you go."

"Okay."

The Eyelid Scales continue moving up and down.

"Oh, Penny, wait!" Dallergut stops her.

"Yes?"

"I forgot to give you an official welcome. Congratulations! We're happy to have you working for us. Hope you like it here so far."

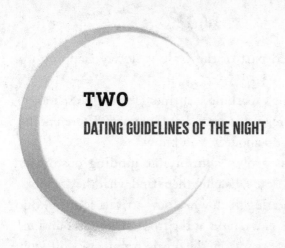

TWO
DATING GUIDELINES OF THE NIGHT

It's been a month, and Penny is adjusting well at the Dallergut Dream Department Store. The most significant improvement is that she now knows all the nitty-gritty details about the Eyelid Scales of the regulars. Specifically, that regular No. 898's scale often struggles to keep its heavy eyelids up, and it happens so frequently that Penny is reasonably sure something's wrong with the scale itself.

"Weather, this scale must be broken. I've been watching it closely, and right now, it's not even nighttime in the time zone where this customer lives, and he has been dozing off from 8:00 a.m. to 5:00 p.m. See here! It's still moving right now!"

The eyelid part of the scale is slowly flapping up and down.

"That scale's working just fine. He's a high schooler, must be dozing off in class. Let him sleep. There's nothing you can do about it, you know."

Penny has grown comfortable guiding customers through the floors, helping them find what they're looking for, or alerting them when new arrivals come in. But one of the essential tasks at the front desk is accounting, which means organizing the dream payments, a difficult job to master. More than anything, she finds handling the Dream Pay Systems program the trickiest. So does Dallergut, so the responsibility falls solely to Weather.

"Dream payments are made with half the emotion a customer feels after they dream," Weather explains. "So, customers who naturally *feel* more have a higher chance of paying more. That's why it's important to take good care of our regulars. Most of their dreams are rich in emotion."

"How is it possible to pay with emotion?"

"That's where the Dream Pay Systems program comes in! It's sort of like IoT technology—you know, Internet of Things? The program connects the customers to our safe. When they pay for their dreams, the currency comes to our safe, and we can read the data from our computers… Penny, are you with me? Can you at least pretend you're following?" Weather pleads.

"Oh, I'm sorry… It's just that… It's hard to visualize it in my head…"

"Well, I guess I'll have to keep doing it myself for the time being."

✷ ✷ ✷

Weather comes to work early each morning, and the first thing she does is take the dream payments from the safe and deposit them at the bank across the street. When Weather's busy with this task, Penny fills in for her at the front desk, which keeps her on her toes.

This morning, Penny is looking around like a meerkat, ready to keep an eye on things while Weather checks the safe. But Weather returns only moments after leaving.

"Are you done already?" Penny asks.

She's sweating profusely, bent over and clutching her stomach. "I think something was off with the omelet I had this morning. L–let me stop by…the restroom… I may be a minute. Can you go to the bank for me? Take the key to the storage room and open the safe with it. You'll see two full glass bottles inside. Take them to the bank counter, and they'll take care of it. Just tell them you're from the Dream Department Store. You sh-should hurry… You'll get caught in the morning rush."

Weather hands a small key to Penny before darting to the restroom.

Penny has no time to panic. She quickly scribbles a note and leaves it on the front desk: "Gone to bank for a while—Penny." As she trots toward the storage room, she mumbles to herself, "The safe, two glass bottles, full, the bank counter, tell them I'm from the Dream Department Store."

Inside the neatly organized storage room is a safe. It is much larger than Penny thought it would be, and she struggles to find the keyhole. She finally locates it by her feet, pushes and twists the key until she hears it unlock. She pulls open the door—as massive as the lobby entrance—and a big room reveals itself, deep like a cave.

The safe looks like a giant spice cabinet in the basement of a wealthy house. Inside each custom-made case are rows of glass bottles, containing different colored liquids: mysterious turquoise, blinding ivory and dusky bloodred. There is something about the bloodred bottle that creeps her out.

The steady dripping of water echoes through the safe. Penny knows these colorful liquids are dream payments, and it is a wonder to witness them in person.

She easily spots the two full glass bottles Weather mentioned. Someone must have taken them out of their cases and placed them in a lower row of the cabinets last night. Both labels say Flutter, and the liquid inside the bottles is baby pink, like cotton candy. Penny wants to take her time looking at the other bottles, but she hasn't forgotten what Weather said about hurrying to the bank. She rushes to remove two bottles and locks the safe behind her.

Penny heads to the bank with the bottles tucked under her armpits. They're relatively heavy and slippery, which makes her sweat. There must be a better way to transport them; Weather probably forgot to tell her.

As she enters the bank, a cool breeze from the air-conditioning greets her. Luckily it's not too crowded. She takes a queue ticket, proud of herself for smoothly carrying out the task up to this point.

No more klutz Penny! I can do things well on my own.

She takes a seat, clutching the glass bottles, the baby pink liquid sloshing inside. Seven people are waiting in front of her. Penny hopes they won't take long, but the customers at the counters seem to be there on complicated tasks and are holding up the queue.

Bored, she rests the bottles on the floor and takes out a magazine from a nearby rack. The title reads *Dream Neuroscience—May*.

Wow, what a catchy title, she thinks sarcastically.

She casually flips to a random page and starts skimming.

PAPER OF THE MONTH:
A STUDY ON DREAM PAYMENTS
AND THEIR RESPECTIVE EMOTIONS

Dr. Reeno's *A Study on Dream Payments and Their Respective Emotions* has been selected as Paper of the Month. Numerous papers on the topic have been published, but Dr. Reeno's piece stands apart for depth of research.

"The point is that the customers are aware they are 'oblivious beings.' They have an objective understanding of themselves. They even know that what they 'remember' is not factual reality but information their brain has reprocessed. Ultimately, the fact that they know 'all experiences will eventually be forgotten' makes every moment a once-in-a-lifetime moment. That is why the emotions they feel after dreaming and their respective dream prices hold special power."

Above is Dr. Reeno's answer to our request to summarize the core message of his two-hundred-page dissertation. Some critics have argued that his paper is more a rehashing of previous studies and lacks originality. But the consensus in academia seems to be that in analyzing nearly three thousand cases over a decade, the scope of Dr. Reeno's work deserves recognition. A full version of his paper is available at the *Dream Neuroscience* official website.

The thought of a two-hundred-page dissertation makes Penny dizzy. She closes the magazine without a second thought. There are still five people waiting in line.

Just then, a man in a neat suit sits down next to Penny and strikes up a conversation. "What captivating color you have in those bottles. Very high quality. Worth at least two hundred gordens, I'd say. Where're you from? I haven't seen you around."

"I'm from the department store across the street. I'm new there, so this would be your first time seeing me." Penny assumes the guy must work for the bank.

"What number are you? There's still time until your turn—how about I show you around?"

Penny is about to decline his offer, pointing at the heavy bottles that have her tethered to her seat, when he picks one up and says, "Let me help you."

Penny finds herself following the man as he guides her past the counters to an area with a huge electronic display board facing about a hundred chairs. It looks like someone just replicated a train station waiting room.

People are nervously looking up at the board, which displays the market prices of different emotions in real time, like stocks in the stock market.

Fulfilled and Confidence are up by fifteen percent in deep red, ranking the highest. Below them are Futility and Lethargy, whose prices are dropping. The people sitting closest to the display board are either desperately clasping their hands in prayer or heaving a deep sigh.

"A beef burger combo is one gorden, and how much

is one bottle of Fulfilled—two hundred?" one guy rants. "It's ridiculous that somebody would pay that much for some nobody's accomplishment just to get vicarious satisfaction from it! Had I hoarded it last year, I'd be long retired by now!"

Penny finds the price for Flutter on the upper line. It is now being traded at 180 gordens per bottle. She realizes she would be in deep trouble if she lost her own bottles. She holds hers tight and turns to the man—only to find him gone.

Gone with the other Flutter bottle he was holding for her.

She *is* in trouble. A chill races down her spine.

Is he a swindler? He must have been roaming around, looking for an unwitting, woolly-headed victim to coin-snatch from, and he happened to catch Penny, who completely fits the bill. What was she thinking to admit she's new? She must've been the perfect, most delicious prey. So naive. She frantically looks around, but he's nowhere to be seen.

She needs to deposit the remaining bottle, but her turn has well passed. To make matters worse, her queue ticket is gone. She can't leave the front desk vacant any longer, so she decides to head back to the store.

Weather is already back at the front desk, looking

more buoyant. Her restroom situation must have been well taken care of—unlike Penny's disaster.

"Weather…"

"What's wrong, Penny? Wait, why did you bring that back?"

Penny explains everything. Now that she is verbalizing what happened, she feels like the dumbest person in the world.

"Gosh, this is bad. Flutter is rare these days. It's my fault. I shouldn't have given you such a big task. I'll tell Dallergut, don't you worry. Maybe we can still catch him if we call the police. That guy tried to scam me a couple of times, too."

"You should've kicked him in the joints back then, Weather," says Dallergut, appearing without warning. "So, what you're saying is, you've been robbed of one dream payment bottle and failed to deposit the other? The Flutter bottle price has reached its peak today, for the first time in three months…"

"I'm so sorry, sir." Penny can barely look Dallergut in the eye.

"But all for the better! I needed a Flutter bottle myself and meant to stop by the front desk to tell Weather not to deposit it, only I forgot. It's a good thing you brought it back for me! Today's working out just fine. As for the lost bottle, let's consider it a price paid for learning the lesson—that the world is a scary place."

Dallergut's generosity make Penny feel even more horrible.

"I am so, so sorry. Where do you want me to put the Flutter?"

"This? I have a feeling a certain customer will visit us today. And she'll need it."

* * *

Ah-young has been a regular at the Dallergut Dream Department Store since she was young. She thought she generally dreamed a lot, but it never occurred to her that she had a go-to dream store to visit every night because everything she dreamed each night would be forgotten by morning.

Ah-young was born in the suburbs, where she grew up and finished college. After that she found work in a metropolitan city and a place to live on her own, close to her typical, nine-to-five office job. She got the job as soon as she graduated, and had been working there for four years now. She was twenty-eight years old and, in theory, her life was smooth sailing.

"There's no one. Literally, no one." Ah-young sighed on the phone.

"Really? Doesn't your company have a lot of guys?"

"All of them are married or taken, or not my type, or I'm not theirs."

"I doubt that! Have you checked every one of them to know that? Or maybe you're not interested in dating in the first place?"

"Honestly, I have no idea where to start. How are you supposed to initiate a date as an adult?"

"So, you do have someone, don't you? I knew it!"

"Well…"

★ ★ ★

Ah-young sprawled out on her queen-size bed after finishing the phone call with her girlfriend. The bed looked especially huge tonight, and it was bugging her.

"Ah, so lonely."

She had reached the point where she verbalized how lonely she was in her room. Her voice made small echoes as it bounced off the walls, which sounded pathetic. It was already around midnight.

Ah-young had worked overtime and then she came straight home, showered, threw out the recycling, had dinner, and then took the short call with her friend. Now she'd only have six hours left to sleep. If she binged You-Tube and a webcomic series through the night again,

she'd be staying up for two nights in a row. Enough
about loneliness, she needed sleep. She had to go to
work tomorrow.

How long will I have to live like this? Ah-young struggled to keep this question out of her mind. It was bad to
think deep thoughts before bed. She knew all too well
from past experiences that it wouldn't help her fall asleep.

She pulled the blanket to her neck and set the alarm
on her smartphone, then checked the weather for tomorrow. Tomorrow's air quality: terrible. Weather: cloudy.
All the icons in the weather app were gray.

*What a grim life. Definitely not how I'd imagined my twen-
ties would look… Nothing colorful.*

Actually, that wasn't entirely true. Ah-young thought
of the guy she'd mentioned to her friend on the call. He
was from a vendor company and visited the office every
Wednesday. After completing his morning tasks, he'd
eat lunch at a one-person table in a restaurant that she
also frequented.

"Hello, this is Jong-seok Hyun from Tech Industries.
Do you have a moment?"

"Yes, hello, this is Ah-young Jeong. I'm available.
How can I help you?"

"I plan to visit at 10:00 a.m. on Wednesday of this
week. Does that time work?"

The two had spoken on work calls before and exchanged a few greetings in person, but that was all. Yet his consistency in calling her every Monday at the same time for confirmation, his upright posture when greeting her in person, and his calm, professional attitude (of course, "professional" was subjective) toward sometimes frustrating and annoying work requests—all of this caught her eye.

And recently, he'd started appearing in her dreams, even more handsome and taller than in real life.

Ah-young reflected on her past, wondering when she'd last developed a relationship from "mere fondness" into something "romantic." *Maybe in high school? Or first year in college? Wait, is tomorrow Wednesday?* Suddenly, she felt the knot in her belly relaxing. She would see him tomorrow.

Ah-young wrapped herself in the blanket and rolled toward the wall. She sincerely hoped he would never find this out about her—that she was tossing and turning, giddy at the thought of him. No doubt it would make him feel uncomfortable, knowing he was being admired at work, and fantasized about at night by a stranger! He could already be married or with someone.

Her fluttering heart was no different from a teenage girl's, but she was at an age where worries and concerns came before romance.

Okay, now I'm overthinking again. I really must go to sleep.

Let me at least have this feeling last longer, even if it's one-sided, Ah-young prayed as she fell asleep.

✷ ✷ ✷

"Weather, I think No. 201 should be here soon."

"Oh, you're right." Weather glances at the Eyelid Scale.

"What a relief. She usually comes every day, so I was worried when she didn't stop by yesterday," Penny says, smiling as she looks at No. 201's Eyelid Scale. The eyelid is completely closed, the pendulum pointing at the bottom, "REM sleep."

The moment Penny finishes talking, No. 201 comes in from the entrance. Penny and Weather greet her with delight.

"Welcome!"

"Hi! I'm here to take the same dream. I've been enjoying it lately."

"Of course. The third floor is pretty hectic now. Let me grab it for you. Please wait here."

Penny rushes upstairs where Mogberry, the third-floor manager, is sorting through new arrivals with other employees. Her baby hair is sticking out in all directions, as usual. Penny weaves through mounds of boxes to reach the Steady Sellers section. Popular dream boxes are stacked on the display. They'd been neatly organized this morning, but now that customers have swept through, they're in disarray.

Penny rummages through the boxes to find the dream the woman's looking for. After sorting past the Leprechauns' "Flying Dream" for the fifth time, Penny finally spots the box with heart-shaped decorations. The ribbon has its dreammaker, Keith Gruer, printed on it. Keith Gruer is a veteran maker of romantic dreams. According to a well-informed source (Assam) Gruer is actually so bad at relationships in his personal life that he has gone through over a hundred breakups. He shaves his head whenever he has a breakup, so no one has ever seen him with long hair. But it is an established truth in the dream industry that the quality of his dreams gets better with every heartbreak.

"Is this the one?" Penny rushes back to the first floor, handing the box to the customer. The box is labeled "Meeting Your Crush."

"Yes, this is it."

"Here you go. Thank you."

"Do I pay later this time too?" the woman asks as she takes the box.

"Yes. As always, all you need to do is share a little piece of your feelings after you wake up. If you don't feel anything after the dream, we won't charge you!" Penny has learned all this from Weather.

The woman quietly leaves the store with the box. Her steps seem light and bouncy, but for some reason, watching her walk away leaves Penny uneasy, and she doesn't know why.

As the day goes by, the crowds thin out. Penny sweeps the floor, lost in thought. Since No. 201's visit, something's been bothering her, but she can't put her finger on it. She mindlessly sweeps until she arrives at Dallergut's office near the staircase. Then she realizes what's bothering her.

"Oh, I'm sorry, I've spilled a lot of crumbs from the cookies, right?" The office door flings wide open as Dallergut trudges out.

"No worries at all, Dallergut. I was just cleaning up in my downtime. But, then…"

"Everything okay?"

"Actually, I have a question about Customer No. 201."

"Oh, 201. She is a long-time regular."

"Do you think it's a good idea to keep selling her 'Meeting Your Crush'?"

"Is there a problem?" Dallergut asks, genuinely interested in Penny's answer.

"Well, I think dreaming about your crush a few times

is fine. But with each new dream the feelings would amplify and lead to more heartache. For her to keep dreaming the same dream…" Penny trails off, momentarily lost in thought. "Right!" She finally realizes what has been bugging her since seeing the customer leave. "It probably means she's stalling out in real life!"

"Penny, do you know what our out-of-town customers generally think dreams are, including No. 201?"

"Of course! I've learned about this. The subconscious. They think dreams are manifestations of their subconscious."

"Yes, that's correct."

"So? What about it?" Penny doesn't get where this is going. She doesn't want to seem like a pumpkin-headed employee, constantly asking questions, but still, her curiosity gets the better of her.

"I'm sure you're aware, but outside customers don't remember anything about their time in our store when they wake up from their dreams. Because of that, the best explanation they can come up with for their dreams is their subconscious. What would you do if you were a customer?"

"If my crush keeps appearing in my dreams, I would think my feelings had grown to the point that even my subconscious is consumed by that person," says Penny, unsure.

"Right. And as time passes, you'd be certain you have strong feelings for that person."

"Yes, but that's the thing. That's not enough to start a romantic relationship. Dreams are just dreams…" Penny thinks of how the woman was so excited to buy the dream again, and her heart aches for her. Still, Dallergut looks merry.

"Love starts when you recognize your feelings. Whether it ends in one-sided or reciprocal love, our job is done here."

"I just hope it's not one-sided. That's too painful."

"As you said, dreams are just dreams, right? Let's keep our hopes high for her in real life."

* * *

Ah-young woke up five minutes before her alarm. Her eyes just opened, feeling refreshed without the help of the alarm. She faintly remembered having gone to a store in her dream, but the more she tried to remember, the more it slipped out of her head, like a grain of sand escaping from her hand. Now, she no longer remembered any of it. All she did remember was that *he* was in her dream, yet again. In the dream, she was with him at his favorite restaurant. She was sitting close to him. He sat in his usual seat; they were having a long conversation. They seemed to have committed to meeting there every day, and the conversation was comfortable, as if they had been together for a long time.

Ah-young got up, the afterglow of the dream still lingering as she headed to the shower. Her heart was indeed aflutter. But, as soon as the showerhead sprayed cold water on her skin, she came to her senses.

What's wrong with me? What's all this fuss?

✳ ✳ ✳

Before the customer's flutter fades, an alarm rings in the lobby on the first floor of the Dallergut Dream Department Store.

Ding Dong. "*Payment received from Customer No. 201. A small amount of Flutter has arrived for 'Meeting Your Crush.'*"

"This system is connected to those bottles in the safe, right?" asks Penny, reading the notification.

"Finally, you're getting it! And yes, the world has definitely evolved for the better. Back in the old days, we spilled more than we collected, trying to transfer the payments into the bottles ourselves. Running around with a scale, trying to weigh them whenever they arrived—it would take up the whole day."

"By the way, what's Dallergut going to do with that one Flutter bottle?"

The bottle that Penny failed to deposit at the bank keeps bugging her. It is still standing on the front desk.

"If Dallergut has something in mind, I'm sure it'll get put to good use," Weather assures her.

✱ ✱ ✱

At work, Ah-young was finding it hard to focus. The more she thought about why she kept dreaming about him every night, the less she could help but reach one conclusion.

Do I have feelings for him?

From the next cubicle, she heard her boss say, "Ah-young, is Jong-seok coming for the meeting today?"

It was 9:55 a.m. He would typically be here by now. He usually arrived exactly ten minutes before the meeting, or he'd call her to let her know he was running late. Ah-young thought it strange—and just then, her desk phone rang.

"Hello, this is Ah-young Jeong from the Tech Support department."

"Hello! This is Jong-seok Hyun from Tech Industries." He sounded like he was panting. As if he'd been running. "I'm sorry, but I left the meeting materials in my car. I should be there by 10:00 a.m."

"Oh, okay." Then, thinking her answer might have been too cold, Ah-young quickly added, "I'll let my manager know. Please take your time."

"Thank you!"

After Ah-young hung up, she fidgeted with the phone cord. He'd sounded uncharacteristically flustered. His voice left her heart skipping a beat again.

Stop. Focus. You're at work. She tried hard to keep it together.

At 10:00 a.m. sharp, the door swung open, and in came Jong-seok. Ah-young pretended not to notice him, but she glanced at him from the corner of her eye. She'd told him not to hurry, but his cheeks were flushed from rushing here.

He kept glancing around as if looking for someone. Then he met her gaze, catching her off guard. Before she could look away, he nodded and smiled widely, revealing dimples on each cheek.

You even have perfect dimples. Not fair!

Ah-young couldn't help but admit it. She was indeed falling for him.

Things had seemed off ever since Jong-seok woke up that morning. His ex-girlfriend appeared in his dream, and he woke up feeling uneasy. They'd dated so long ago that he no longer remembered what had caused the breakup, and the dream didn't trigger any regrets or longing. It just made him uncomfortable that she'd made an appearance. And she'd been appearing more often recently.

What a troubling subconscious I have.

That morning, Jong-seok was so lost in thought that he forgot his meeting materials in the car. He hated being late for meetings. He was turning thirty soon, and he didn't want to enter a new decade with no dating life and an incompetent work life.

As he rushed back to the parking lot, he made a phone call. After a couple of rings and a *click*, the woman from the client's office answered.

"Hello, this is Ah-young Jeong from the Tech Support department."

"Hello! This is Jong-seok Hyun from Tech Industries." He was worried his panting voice would sound comical to her. *How pathetic.* He raised his voice to try and cover his heavy breathing. "I'm sorry, but I left the meeting materials in my car. I should be there by 10:00 a.m."

"Oh, okay." Her response was short. But before hanging up, she added, "I'll let my manager know. Please take your time."

"Thank you!" Her response gave him the boost of cheer he needed to get through the day.

✳ ✳ ✳

That night, Jong-seok went to bed exhausted. He fell asleep as soon as his head hit the pillow.

✳ ✳ ✳

"Welcome!" Penny immediately recognizes the man. Recently, he's been buying the same dream, "Meeting an Ex-Girlfriend," from the Memories section on the second floor. "Are you looking for the same dream?"

"Yes, please," he replies blankly.

Before Penny goes to the second floor, Dallergut intervenes. "Sir, I don't think you need that dream anymore."

"Excuse me?"

"You might not remember this, but you begged me two years ago for dreams in which an ex-girlfriend appears."

"Did I...? If it was two years ago... It must have been right after we broke up."

"Yes. And you'd always wake up in tears, right?"

"Yes, I used to. But I was okay soon after. And I didn't dream about her for a long time." He stops, as if considering this. "But wait, why am I dreaming about her again now?"

"Because you asked me to give you a dream about her again when you were ready to start a new relationship. You wanted to make sure you were really over her first. So I suggested that same dream, 'Meeting an Ex-Girlfriend.'"

"I see."

"And you haven't been paying for your dreams. That means, you no longer have feelings for your ex-girlfriend, even in your dreams."

"It also means our dreams have gone to waste," Weather adds.

"That's right. We're afraid we can no longer sell that dream to you. You won't have feelings to pay us back with, anyway," Dallergut says.

"Okay then," the man responds as he turns to leave. He seems to feel awkward.

"But before you go, can I offer you a nice drink? The night is long. Why hurry?" Dallergut's friendly tone stops the man, and he turns back. Dallergut produces the Flutter bottle from the front desk and opens the cork. Pink smoke rises from within. Dallergut pours a teacup full of liquid and hands it to the man.

"Go ahead. Drink it up."

The man finishes the drink and leaves the store looking much more cheerful than he did when he came in, before disappearing into thin air.

"Dallergut, why did you give all that expensive Flutter away?" Penny asks in frustration. *He just threw it away—what a waste.*

"You said one-sided love is too painful," Dallergut says.

Penny's mouth falls open. "Is *he* No. 201's crush?"

Dallergut nods shortly and firmly, confused as to why she bothers to ask such an obvious question.

"How did you know?"

"When you run a store for three decades, you just know."

✶ ✶ ✶

Jong-seok woke up feeling more refreshed than ever. He was giddy, his heart full of excitement. *Today's a good day to start something new*, he thought. He kept his phone plugged into the charger, humming as he headed into the shower.

The sound of splashing water mixed with his singing. Then his phone dinged with a text. Only the first part of the message appeared on the locked screen.

New Message: Hi, this is Ah-young Jeong. Hope you remember me...?

* * *

"So, how did you meet your boyfriend?"

"I had a crush on him. I just went ahead and asked him out."

"Really? You don't seem the type."

"I know. But when your feelings are urgent, you change."

"Weren't you afraid of rejection?"

"I was more afraid of coming off as weird to him. I met him at work."

"Wow, you must've really liked him."

"After I sent that first text I immediately turned off my phone. I was worried he would never get back to me. I waited for about two hours and turned it back on. He called me out later for almost ghosting him. But he had asked me out."

"So, looking back now, do you think you made the right choice?"

"Of course! It's one of the top-five best decisions I've ever made. Maybe even top three."

THREE
PRECOGNITIVE DREAM

It's a sunny day in July. Penny has been working at the Dallergut Dream Department Store for three months. The streets are full of merchants opening their shops for the day, and the Noctilucas scurry around, collecting the rented sleepwear people have dumped everywhere. Penny is heading to work, sipping on a soy latte she bought at a coffee shop. By the time she arrives at the store, she realizes she's much earlier than usual.

All employees at the Dallergut Dream Department Store have their shifts carefully assigned so the store can be run twenty-four seven unless dreams sell out. There is no point in coming in early. Penny decides to enjoy the sun outside. She looks up at the five-story wooden building towering over the center of the city. The Dal-

lergut Dream Department Store. The sight of it is indeed
a marvel to behold when she's not at work. But her re-
spite doesn't last long.

"Hey, Penny, glad you're early. Hurry up and come
help us!"

The entrance bursts open, revealing Vigo Myers, the
second-floor manager, shouting at Penny. He holds a
half-squished peach in one hand and fans himself with
the other.

"Oh… O-okay!" answers Penny, feeling flustered as
she enters the store.

The entire store smells of tart fruit. Decorations made
of peaches, apricots, big green grapes and other fruits are
hanging around the lobby. Penny would easily mistake
it for a random orchard if there were no familiar faces.

Besides Vigo Myers, other employees have been temporarily reassigned from each floor to hang fruit, decorate leaves and clean up fallen fruit from the ground.
Among them are some unexpected workers.

"Motail, could you please send the Leprechauns back
to their own store? Why in the world are they here?"
the third-floor manager, Mogberry, shouts.

"I asked them to come. I thought, why should I have
to climb up the ladder when we have flying friends next
door? Plus they happily obliged. Just look at them—

they're working so hard for us!" Motail points at the ceiling.

Above them, pairs of Leprechauns are struggling to hang green grapes as big as their bodies. At least five of the grapes have dropped around Penny. One even falls on a passing customer.

"Ouch!"

"Oh dear, we're so sorry! Are you okay? Do you mind going upstairs? As you can see, the lobby is a bit chaotic at the moment." Weather apologizes on their behalf.

"What *are* all these?" Penny picks up one of the fallen green grapes.

"You didn't hear? We're expecting a VIP today," Mogberry says, folding a fruit box in half. Her hair looks especially disheveled, with even more baby hair sticking out than usual.

"Who is this VIP we're all decorating the place for—"

Penny's question is interrupted by Mogberry's strict command. "Can you take these out? What would Madam Rockabye think if she saw this? These are long expired!" She moves on from the fruit boxes and starts cleaning up the heaps of dream boxes in the lobby.

Penny rolls up her sleeves to help Mogberry. Her unfinished soy latte on the front desk has gone cold. She makes a mental note that next time she gets to work early, she won't hang around in front of the store.

"Mogberry, don't throw them all away! I'll take them. They'll sell well on the fifth floor with big discounts!" Motail unabashedly intervenes, munching on the left-over green grapes. The Leprechauns are flying around him in their sleeveless shirts and adorable leather vests, each nibbling on a single grape in their arms.

"Oh, Motail, please. I know you sell dreams at a discount, but this is pushing it too far. The dreams would be undreamable, with chunks of scenes, smell and color all gone. If you have any decency, you can't sell these. Dallergut would be so furious if he found out. And if Babynap Rockabye discovers we're selling such low-quality work… I don't even want to imagine how she'd react. She'd never do business with us again."

"But the customers won't remember a thing about their dreams…"

"That's right, I second that!" the Leprechauns chime in. They seem inclined to add more, but Mogberry's furious glare cuts them short.

Penny picks up the name from their conversation. "Babynap Rockabye, you said? She's the one who's coming today?"

"Yes, for the first time in years. That's why we've been decorating the store. She loves sweet and tart fruit. I heard she's bringing mounds of dreams at Dallergut's special request! I can't wait to see them! Definitely one of the perks of working here. When else would I ever get to meet her in person?"

Babynap Rockabye is one of the Legendary Big Five, and she's won more than ten Grand Prix prizes at the year-end awards. She's the only director who creates conception dreams, and she's a long beloved public figure. Penny has only ever seen her in magazines and on television. She never imagined she'd meet her in person.

"That's it, guys. This should be enough, so whoever is done with their shifts can leave. Didn't think it would be this big a hassle."

Dallergut, who Penny had thought was in his office, sticks his neck out from piles of empty boxes. He's wearing a working jacket instead of his go-to T-shirt and cardigan. The baggy outerwear makes him look slight.

"You were here all along?" Penny asks, clearing up the boxes that are blocking his view.

"It was my idea to decorate the lobby for Babynap. I just thought a few fake fruits would do, and now it's out of control! Hey, guys! You can leave! Now. Off you go!" Dallergut rubs his neck with a grimace.

But no one budges at Dallergut's command. Everyone is frozen, staring at the lobby door.

Penny follows their gaze and her eyes alight upon a petite old lady, standing at the entrance with her entourage.

Penny immediately realizes why everyone's frozen.

The incredible aura this frail old lady exudes leaves them speechless. Babynap Rockabye. Her mysterious, other-worldly energy seems to make time run back and forth around her. She moves as if in slow motion, and yet before Penny can gather her bearings, Babynap Rockabye is already inside the store.

"Babynap! Good to see you!" Dallergut greets her.

"Oh, my dear old friend. I haven't seen you since last year's general assembly. My, my! Love the smell of this fruit. The store feels…blissful," Rockabye marvels at the spectacle of the fruit dangling around the lobby.

Dallergut and Babynap Rockabye shake hands. Awe-struck, the other employees cover their mouths at the sight of her.

Penny is fortunate to be standing near her. Rock-abye's scent is richer and stronger than the decorative fruit around them. Her warm countenance is a mix of wrinkles and plump, rosy cheeks like a baby's.

Rockabye's entourage follows her into the store, each of them holding heavy bundles wrapped in high-end silk.

"Here you go, Dallergut, as promised. They are not my best products, but I trust you'll take good care of them. As you always do."

"Nonsense, they are our most precious products! Thank you for choosing our store," Dallergut says, holding up one of the bundles.

Penny is too curious about what's unfolding around her to stay quiet.

"Mogberry, are they all conception dreams? I thought conception dreams were only made to order. Are we allowed to have them premade?"

Mogberry seems too carried away with the silk bundles to hear her.

"Hello? Mogberry? What I'm trying to get at is that someone must be pregnant first to get a conception dream, correct? How are you supposed to know who will be pregnant in order to have the dreams premade?"

The more questions Penny asks, the more confused she becomes. Come to think of it, the idea of a conception dream itself doesn't make sense. People usually have conception dreams before they even realize they're pregnant. *How is that possible?*

"Those aren't technically conception dreams," Mogberry replies, too spellbound by the silk bundles to look up at her. "They're leftovers from the productions."

"Leftovers? What's the use?"

Now, Mogberry turns to her. "Back to your other question: how do we know who will be pregnant?" She narrows her eyes, pausing for dramatic effect.

"Right. It doesn't make sense if you think about it. Foretelling the future by dreaming that a baby will be born...?" Penny feels confused.

"That's exactly what this is about. Foretelling the future."

"I'm sorry?"

"Conception dreams are precognitive dreams. The dreammaker foresees that a baby will be conceived in advance and premakes a dream accordingly."

"Precognitive dreams?" Penny asks in disbelief.

"I can't say for sure, but rumor has it that Babynap Rockabye is one of the distant descendants of the First Disciple. You know, the disciple who ruled over the future in the tale of *The Time God and the Three Disciples*? You've surely read the story. Anyway, it's not necessarily the case that every descendant has prophetic visions, but they can often glimpse snippets of the future or get a sense of big events. And they can especially sense the seeds of new life more strongly than anything else. That's how Babynap Rockabye can create these conception dreams. Isn't that amazing?"

"So you're saying they're...?" Penny points at Rockabye's bundles.

"Yes. They may be leftovers, but they are still precognitive dreams indeed!"

"Unbelievable!"

In short, Penny is not only at a historical moment where the descendants of the First and Third Disciples are conversing, she's also witnessing piles of precognitive dreams within her arm's reach. It is like she's been dropped into a fairy tale.

Are they really precognitive dreams? Will I be able to see my own future? Penny starts imagining her future husband, her mouth agape.

"Are you leaving already? That's too soon," Dallergut says to Rockabye, cutting Penny's daydreaming short.

"I have many couples waiting for my dreams. I must get going. I'll see you at the next meeting in a few months. It was nice seeing you, Dallergut, and thank you all for this. You guys must have put in a lot of work for this old lady." Babynap Rockabye smiles as she looks at the hanging fruits, then at the entire staff, who nod their heads in gratitude.

"Please take these fruits with you, then," Dallergut says, and Rockabye's entourage gather the decorations and neatly pack them up.

"We should've just handed them the fruit in boxes in the first place. Would have saved us the hassle, and the dirty floor," mutters Vigo Myers, wiping the peach juice from his hand with his handkerchief.

After Babynap Rockabye and her entourage are gone, the lobby quickly returns to normal, thanks to the help of the second-floor employees, who have outdone themselves by pitching in. Dallergut finally manages to send back the rest of the staff, although they can hardly keep their eyes off the pile of dream boxes Rockabye has left. Dallergut starts sorting out the bundles with Weather and Penny.

"I still can't believe my eyes. Are they really…?"

"You want the dream, too, huh?"

"Oh, Weather, of course! So does everybody else on the planet!" Penny raises her voice excitedly.

They take the dream boxes from the silk bundles and arrange them on the displays and counters. Penny carefully writes out a notice: *Select Precognitive Dreams in Stock.*

In a matter of hours, Penny finds herself stuck between a line of customers drooling over the precognitive dreams and Dallergut, who seldom sells them. Usually, Dallergut would go straight to his office, but this time he hangs around the dream products, hampering sales.

"One precognitive dream—actually, two, please," one customer asks.

"May I ask why you want to see your future?" Dallergut asks.

"Do I have to share that?"

"We need to make sure these go to those in need. As you know, there are only a handful of them."

"I want to know the lottery numbers for this week."

"We're sorry, but we don't sell them for that use."

"What? You asked me. Are you screening customers?" The patron fumes.

Penny becomes anxious and quickly tries to draw the customer's attention to another dream. "How about this one? It's about an apocalypse where the earth is destroyed, and you're the last human standing. What an experience, don't you think?"

"I'm good," the customer curtly replies, still furious as he leaves the store.

Another customer wants to see his future wife, and another wants to know when she'll finally pass the civil service exam. Dallergut turns them both down.

"Looks like we're not going to sell any today," Penny mumbles.

"Let's give it some time." Weather shrugs it off.

"Why is Babynap Rockabye doing business with Dallergut? He doesn't seem to be trying to boost her sales," Penny says, trying not to sound like she's talking behind his back.

"Rockabye doesn't think her dreams are worth all the fuss. She didn't choose us as her only store because she's being picky. She's just selling to her old friend Dallergut, thinking her dreams are too embarrassing for the public in the first place."

"No way. They're precognitive dreams, for God's sake. She's too humble."

"If you could pick and choose the future you want to see, maybe. But not even she can make that possible. She can only show a snippet of the future, at most. A very short slice, like a split second."

"Still, it's amazing to foresee the future."

"Is it really? What if you don't get the information you're hoping for? What if you only see a random scene of a child dropping a baseball, or a mundane slice-of-life moment where you're just staring at your black tea boiling? Would you still think it's amazing?"

"Well… Not something that mundane."

"Those dreams are all mundane. But they can become special to someone if we sell them to the right person." Weather smiles mischievously, putting on the same expression Dallergut often wears. Penny is beginning to understand how they've kept their work partnership going for over thirty years.

Meanwhile, Dallergut keeps guard over the precognitive dream display, still shooing customers away. He seems in no rush.

★ ★ ★

Na-rim was an aspiring screenwriter. She'd been working part-time at a movie theater for a long time. It was the best part-time job she could ever wish for because she could watch movies for free and brood over the dialogue or eavesdrop on people sharing raw feedback.

"Thank you. Enjoy your day!" Na-rim was bidding farewell to moviegoers at the exit. Two people, likely a couple, were the last to leave.

"What'd you think? I thought it was decent," said one of them.

"Wasn't it too predictable?" said the other. "So many clichés, it's like I've seen this before with a different cast. The theme felt too conventional, as well."

Na-rim nodded in solid agreement. She imagined how the story would have played out if she had been the writer. As she cleaned up leftover popcorn beneath arm-rests, all she thought about were ideas for her own stories.

Na-rim wanted her first script to be a romantic comedy. She loved the bubbly rom-com posters and cute, familiar titles.

In fact, romantic inspirations were all around her. She'd heard Employee A from the cafeteria and Employee B from the ticket counter were secretly seeing each other. She'd also heard an interesting story about C, who made the best grilled butter squid, and D, who worked in the parking lot. But they needed to be more exceptional to feature in a movie. Na-rim struggled to develop an ordinary idea into something special.

"Hey, what are you doing tonight?" a fellow part-timer asked, as she helped Na-rim clean up nacho crumbs.

"I'm having dinner with a friend from high school. You?"

"Actually, I booked a session at a fortune-teller's shop nearby. Heard they're great. I'm just a bit nervous about going alone, so I was wondering if you wanted to tag along. I remember you said you're an aspiring screenwriter. Don't you want to know if you will become a successful writer? Maybe you could join me in the next session. How does that sound?"

"I'm good, thanks," Na-rim said, and seeing the coworker pout, she smiled and added, trying to appease her, "I mean, what fun is it if you know your future in advance?"

* * *

When Na-rim met her friend for dinner, the friend's eyes were twinkling. Because Ah-young, her best friend for more than a decade, had just started dating someone.

"So, you're saying the guy kept appearing in your dreams?"

"For several nights in a row! It made me think I must really be into him."

"And that made you ask him out first? You, Ah-young Jeong, the infamous hard to get?"

"I thought the odds were better than doing nothing at all. Pride doesn't pay the bills."

"That's badass. So, you're officially going out with him?"

"Yeah, since last week. I still can't believe it."

"You know, this might just make for good rom-com material if I can polish it up a little."

"It's a fun story for girls' night out for sure, but a screenplay? It's too bland to be movie material."

"Maybe it's because it's been ages since I've been in a relationship. Everyone's dating life feels like a movie to me." Na-rim stirred the now-stale curry on her plate, heaving a sigh.

They each headed back home after dinner.

Na-rim lay in her steel-frame bed.

Is there any good material for a story?

✱ ✱ ✱

"Welcome!" calls Dallergut.

"Welcome to our store," Penny says in a worn-out voice that contrasts with Dallergut's lively one. Three hundred customers came in for precognitive dreams today, and Dallergut sent them all back empty-handed. Penny is exhausted.

"What kind of dream are you looking for?" she asks.

"I'm looking for something fun. If it gives me a story inspiration, even better."

The customer skims through the Limited Releases corner. Piles of precognitive dreams are in plain sight, but she doesn't seem to care. Instead, she methodically picks through unsold dreams clumsily thrown into piles. Penny realizes Dallergut is keeping a close eye on this customer.

Sure enough, he approaches her and strikes up a conversation. "So, you said you're working on a screen-writing contest?"

"Excuse me, do we know each other?" the customer asks back.

"I remember everyone who's been here."

"Oh, I'm sorry. I actually don't remember if I've ever been here before."

"Of course you might not remember, but it doesn't matter. In fact, you've bought pretty much all the dreams we have in stock over the last two years."

The customer's eyebrows flinch as she tries to remember. "I guess so, now that you say that. But I assume none has been story-worthy. I still haven't written a good one," she says, looking disappointed.

"Actually, there's one dream you haven't tried that might interest you..."

"What is it?"

"It's..." Dallergut pauses for a beat to create a dramatic buildup. "A precognitive dream."

"No, thanks—I'm good." The customer rejects his offer right away.

"Don't you want to dream about your future?" Penny asks, curious.

"It's no fun to know things in advance. Same with cinema, same with life. I hate spoilers."

"You don't want to know if you'll be a successful screenwriter?"

"Not at all. I would actually be unhappy to know it in advance. Even if my future seems bright, it's not guaranteed that the dream will come true, and it'll only make me idle. And if it doesn't come true, I would be devastated."

"People are usually curious to know their final destination. You're not?" Weather chimes in. Penny notices that both Weather and Dallergut look rather intrigued.

"My final destination? I don't think humans are some self-driving car, racing toward a finish line. We need to own our lives, start the engine ourselves and sometimes put on the brakes. My life isn't all about becoming a famous writer. I enjoy writing scripts, that's all. Wherever I end up in life, whether beach or desert, I'll embrace it."

Dallergut is looking at her intently.

"I'm sorry—I was rambling." The customer scratches the tip of her nose, seeming a bit embarrassed.

"No, not at all. I'm actually impressed. So, you think if you live in the present, the future will follow accordingly."

"Exactly! That's what I meant," she says confidently.

Dallergut smiles. "In that case, I can't recommend this precognitive dream highly enough. Rest assured, you won't see future events you don't want to see. You'll see an instant of the future, a glimpse, which you'll quickly forget anyway."

"What's the point if I won't remember it?"

"Well, you may remember it someday. You have nothing to lose. As usual, you can pay afterward."

"This looks expensive… How can you be sure that I'll pay?"

"You've always paid your dues. You're a sensitive and emotional customer, and we owe you a great deal. Penny, could you pass her that precognitive dream?"

After a while, the customer leaves the store, tilting her head to examine the dream that Penny handed to her.

"You used reverse psychology, didn't you?" Penny says to Dallergut, who's dusting the display.

"You don't like my sales method?"

"You're selling the dream to those who don't want it, instead of those who'd kill to buy it."

"Rockabye's precognitive dreams can be disappointing to someone who wants to see their future. But they can come as a pleasant surprise to those who have no expectations at all."

"I don't understand."

"You will eventually, when you've worked here long enough—like me."

"I was wondering when you would say that." Penny pouts.

* * *

Na-rim had had a short precognitive dream, but she didn't remember a thing the next day. After brooding over script ideas for a week, she finally decided to use Ah-young's story as her inspiration; it was stuck in her head for some reason.

"Are you sure this will be enough material?" Ah-young asked.

"Of course! The man in your dreams. How romantic!"

"I still feel it's too boring, even though I'm sure you'd polish the dialogues and characters and stuff."

Na-rim and Ah-young were at the curry house again, discussing Na-rim's new screenplay idea over dinner. They were each lost in thought, trying to come up with additional ideas to make the story unique.

Na-rim smudged the leftover carrots on her plate with a fork, while Ah-young fidgeted with her table mat. Just then, Ah-young's phone rang. The name "Jong-seok" came up on the phone screen. Na-rim was present, calmly taking in every detail around her.

And right at that moment, a backstory sprung into her mind, and a strange but clear sense of déjà vu enraptured her.

The soggy leftover carrots, the shape of the table mat's folds from Ah-young's fidgeting, the name appearing on the phone screen… Na-rim knew immediately that the name belonged to Ah-young's boyfriend, despite never having heard his name.

"Boyfriend?" Na-rim asked quietly. Ah-young nodded and took the call.

Na-rim felt the puzzle pieces of the story scattered inside her head suddenly fall into place.

"Déjà vu!" she shouted excitedly as Ah-young hung up the phone.

"Huh?"

"I think I just had a déjà vu! The exact moment when your boyfriend was calling you—I think I already saw it in a dream!"

"Really? That's interesting!"

Na-rim felt a stream of brilliant ideas rushing through

her. As if a finished script had been in her head all along. A string of thoughts began to flow.

"What if I write about someone who can foresee others falling in love in her dreams, and she becomes a dating consultant? Just like how I saw Jong-seok's name in advance in my dream. A consultant with a miserable dating life herself, who can foresee others' love lives from precognitive dreams."

* * *

Ding Dong. "Payment received from Customer No. 1011. A small amount of Flutter has been paid for 'Precognitive Dream.'"

"Weather, look! Remember those precog dreams we sold last week? People have started paying!"

"Really? That's great news. Oh, it's about time Rockabye comes back to collect her dues. I should start converting the payments into cash."

There had been more customers who had come in with no interest in precognitive dreams but then left with a box or two of them at Dallergut's advice.

Ding Dong. "A small amount of Wonder has been paid for 'Precognitive Dream.'"

Ding Dong. "A small amount of Curiosity has been paid for 'Precognitive Dream.'"

"The payments are so diverse. Look, there's Wonder and Curiosity, too!" Penny says.

"Let me see," says Dallergut, intrigued. He has been cleaning the Eyelid Scales behind her. "That's amazing! I told you, it's the customer's call to decide whether a dream is useful." He scrolls through the screen, clicking the mouse to check each notification message.

"Dallergut, I think I just saw an update notification pop up… You didn't just turn that off, did you? I told you we must keep the system up-to-date and always check for any viruses," Weather asks, suspicious.

"There are just too many of them…"

"What?"

"Nothing, Weather…" Dallergut trails off.

"What's 'déjà vu,' by the way?" Penny finds a new word from the product reviews that have come in with the payments. "All the customers are saying they had an amazing 'déjà vu' experience."

"Déjà vu! It means, 'something you've already seen.' It refers to an uncanny sensation that you've experienced something before, even when you know you never have. Isn't it wonderful? Our customers have given our left-over precognitive dreams such an adorable name. How creative is that?" Dallergut exclaims.

"But you know what? Most of them initially marvel

at their déjà vu, but soon shrug it off as a neurological illusion," Weather adds.

"Really? That's disappointing. All that effort we put in to sell the precog dreams, only to get that reaction..." Penny feels discouraged, scratching the back of her head.

"That's the point!" Dallergut chuckles. "No one was confused, even after seeing their future!"

"Of course they weren't, because they didn't technically *see* anything," Penny answers, not understanding what Dallergut's trying to get at.

"That's exactly what we need." Dallergut smiles as he gets up. "I'm thirsty. I'm getting myself something cool to drink. Oh, shall I add a few drops of the fresh Curiosity that just came in today?" With that, Dallergut disappears into the storage room with a glass in his hand.

"This is why Babynap Rockabye brings her leftover productions to our store only. Other stores don't take them, because they have no idea how to sell them," Weather whispers.

Penny recalls the way Dallergut waited for the right customers instead of handing out the dreams to everybody. For a split second, she wonders if Dallergut can foresee the future himself.

"I want to pick Dallergut's brain," Penny mutters.

Dallergut returns from the storage room. "I've put in a couple of drops of fresh Curiosity. Here, give it a try," he says, handing over crystal-blue lemonade that looks like it just came from the deep ocean.

Penny takes the glass and gulps away. A roller coaster of tangy sweetness fills her mouth. Curiosity feels much more pleasant than she'd expected. She feels a sudden surge of motivation.

"Dallergut, I want to do some research on Babynap Rockabye's dreams. I have so many questions," she says, inspired. "And who knows—if I dig deep enough, I might be able to create precog dreams myself and predict things far ahead. Just like in the old tales!"

"Well, it's your choice if you want to study them… But it shouldn't come as a surprise that many people have wasted their lives on that same line of research, if you know what I mean," Dallergut says ambiguously. "There is no such future as grand as you might imagine. There's only the excitement of the present and dreams for tonight."

With that, he disappears into the crowd of customers, the lemonade in his hand.

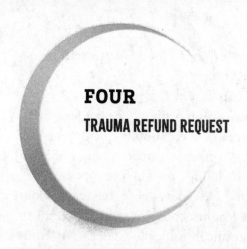

FOUR
TRAUMA REFUND REQUEST

Penny and Weather are in the staff lounge after a late lunch, enjoying a break for the first time in a while.

"Don't worry about the front desk, I'll take care of it," Dallergut had told them. "Go ahead and take a break."

Penny leans back on the old couch, stretching.

Some other staff members have brought their lunch from home, and are sitting around a long table, sluggishly picking at their food as they chat. They're wearing brooches with the number "4" engraved on them. Penny tries to eavesdrop, wondering if they're talking about the rumor that has been circulating among the staff. But they're not.

"I'm eating as slowly as possible so we don't have to

get back to the fourth floor so soon," says a staff member in a low-spirited tone.

"Speedo's work trip should've lasted forever…"

"He just came back this morning… And it feels like a year has gone by already," says another, picking up one grain of fried rice at a time with chopsticks, and then dropping them as the lounge door swings open.

"There you all are!" In comes Speedo, the fourth-floor manager. He's in a bright neon jumpsuit. He seems to have the same jumpsuit in multiple colors. "My floor staff! Good thing I have company for my lunch! Enjoying some egg-fried rice? Consider adding some meat or celery when you fry your rice. I mean, you barely have anything in it. Oh wait, your lunch box isn't a Thermos brand? I bought mine for just one gorden and ninety-nine seals. You know what? Let me share the link to the online shop. You're welcome." Speedo spills words at breakneck speed as the fourth-floor staff calmly close their lunch boxes. "What, are you already done?" Speedo asks.

"I'm not hungry."

"There's, like, half a meal left in your lunch box."

"Just wanted to get back to work. If you'd let us, please…?"

"That's wonderful… Of course. I'll be back up soon."

Before they leave, the staff members cast a desperate

look at Penny and Weather, wordlessly imploring them to keep Speedo company for at least ten more minutes.

"So, Speedo, how was your trip? I heard you spent two weeks at the Nap Research Center. Must've been very educational," Weather says.

"Oh hey, Weather! And Penny! You're still following Weather everywhere like a baby chick," Speedo says, taking a seat as he unwraps his triangle kimbap. "As for the research center, I already knew everything about their research. I had nothing to learn there. I ended up giving them a few tips, actually."

Speedo continues to talk as he eats, shooting rice grains all over the table. Penny leans back. "Take your time to eat, Speedo. Don't you like eating alone, by the way? You always complained about how others can't keep up with your eating pace. Why'd you decide to come to the lounge?"

"Well, you know, at the research center, I always had lunch with the staff there, and they talked a lot about investment and finances, which I found so amusing. So, I grew to love having company at lunch. By the way, Weather, are you interested in investing in cheap emotions?"

"Investing in emotions? How?" asks Weather, looking intrigued.

Penny feigns disinterest, but she's paying close attention too. She's still scared of returning to the bank after the Flutter incident, but now that she has a full-time job, she's more interested in investment.

"You do know that Rage goes up by thirty gordens per bottle in the winter...?"

"Of course I do. A few drops of Rage in the stove will flare up a dying fire. Lasts for at least a week. Nothing better for saving on the heating bills." Weather gives Speedo a thumbs-up. "My husband and I love munching on ice cream near the blazing fire."

"Listen up. The point is you no longer need to spend thirty gordens on Rage! The staff at the research center told me that now is the time to buy Confusion from the bank. Its rate will soar before winter comes."

"But what use is there for Confusion?" Weather asks.

"You can use as much of the gas boiler as you want instead of the old fire stove. You put a few drops of Confusion inside the gas pipe, and the air in the room warms up in a flash. It's like, the air particles just spread out everywhere. The staff gave me the heads-up to buy it in advance because they plan to publish a paper about it soon, which they think will cause a price spike."

"That sounds a bit strange," Penny chimes in. "Doesn't air spread anyway? Sounds like they're making that up. Also, isn't it kind of dangerous to meddle with the gas pipe?" she adds, worried. "You haven't already bought it up, have you?"

"Wh-what if I did?! Chunks of it, for one gorden per bottle. Are you suggesting the research center staff pranked me? Why would they? There's no reason to, they like me!"

Penny has a lot to say but decides not to.

"Speedo, why don't we go back to the bank tomorrow and exchange all of that for cash," says Weather, trying to comfort him. "I can go with you. Don't be disappointed, it was worth a try. Some bad emotions can be very useful indeed."

Speedo slowly stands up, sweeping rice grains off his jumpsuit. "But I do feel like it will go up… How about I wait just a little bit? Even two gordens per bottle will make a huge profit…"

Weather firmly shakes her head. Speedo turns sullen and trudges out of the lounge. Penny and Weather stand too, ready to go back to the front desk.

"Weather, talking about bad emotions got me thinking… Is there any use for bad dreams?" Penny casually asks as she tidies up the cushions on the couch. She's been waiting for the right time to ask about the rumor among the staff.

"What bad dreams?"

"You know… Dreams about your biggest fears, so-called 'nightmares.'"

"Are you asking this because of the new deal?" Weather immediately reads Penny's intention.

"So, you do know! There's a rumor that Dallergut made a deal with a back-alley nightmare dreammaker. Is that true?"

"Yes, it is. His name is Maxim. We should expect his products soon on the third floor."

"But I heard Maxim makes only scary dreams in his pitch-dark office… What if we lose our customers and sales go down?"

"Well. I'm not sure what Dallergut is up to, either… But I'm guessing it'll cause a stir."

★ ★ ★

The news is playing on an electronic display board above the building. The streets are packed but strangely quiet. An eerie silence, as if everyone is on mute, except for the anchor. A man is aimlessly walking along the street when he looks up at the display board. The anchor's voice travels right into his ears, loud and clear, walking straight into his thoughts.

"We're now at a 'demographic cliff,' where the mortality rate is triple the birth rate. We've hit the lowest number of military enlistments. The Military Manpower Administration announces the reenlistment of the discharged under thirty years of age and requires physical checkups once again…"

Feeling overwhelmed, the man winces and closes his eyes. He turns twenty-nine this year and was already discharged from the army seven years ago.

Reenlistment? He opens his eyes again, trying to concentrate on the news, trying to process all this, but he is already in the next scene.

✷ ✷ ✷

The man is at the Military Manpower Administration office in his loose-fitting T-shirt. Inside his dream, he doesn't find this quick scene transition strange. Instead, what fills his mind is the brutal reality of having to go through the military all over again. He's surrounded by other men waiting for their physicals. They're jostling him from side to side, slowly leading him to the front. The other men seem buoyant for some reason.

"I hope I can be on the A-plus rank."

"Me, too. I might as well stay there as long as possible. I'm a total military guy."

What is all this nonsense? The thought stays in his mind, muddying his brain, then disappears.

The man tries his hardest to maneuver his way out of the office, but his feet won't budge an inch. It frustrates him so much that he feels like he's going mad. He clenches his jaw and tries to move, but to no avail.

And just like that, his turn is called. He can't help but watch through his physical checkup, unable to utter a word.

A-plus.

The word *plus* after *A* deeply irritates him. It is good to know he's healthy, but this is the worst way to find out.

* * *

Another scene transition, and now the man is sitting on a leather chair at an old, stinky barbershop. Once again, he can't move; it's as if his body is tied up. He just manages to lift a finger and pulls on the leather part of the armrest where it's starting to come apart at the seams. When it's fully torn, the texture of the cotton wad feels real. The man looks at the barber in the mirror with an anxious look.

"You said you've been selected as A-plus? That's three years of service, right? What a patriot! This is my treat!" says the barber.

The man feels like he'll implode from a reality he cannot escape. Everyone seems strangely relaxed and compliant amid all this nonsense. His own helpless body is languid, unlike his tense emotions.

There's no way I'm going back to the military. There is no way all these discharged men will comply with this madness!

The man's thoughts search for a way out until he reaches a plausible conclusion.

"This must be a dream! Right? Is this a dream?" he asks the barber desperately.

"A dream? Ha ha, you must've had a rough meal." The barber grins and presses an electric razor to his scalp. The cold metal sends chills down his spine, and soon his hair starts falling, and his back is sweating buckets.

Oh, God. This—this is real.

His shirt is soaking wet; he can feel it sticking to the back of the overstuffed leather chair.

* * *

That was when the man woke up from the dream. His bed was drenched with sweat. He blurted out a few pent-up curse words and let "real" reality envelop him.

Thank goodness. That was indeed a dream.

Looking back, none of the scenes in the dream made sense. But when you're inside a dream, you fall for the illusion. *I was discharged long ago; why am I still having these dreams?* The man sluggishly rose and aired his sweaty blanket out the window, but he couldn't shake his unsettled emotions.

✳ ✳ ✳

The woman is a high-school student in her dream tonight. She knows she's in a predicament: It's three days before final exams.

The first day of exams will cover math, chemistry and physics—subjects for which last-minute cramming won't work. *Why did I not study at all?* the woman inside the dream wonders.

And that's the problem. She hasn't studied. She doesn't even recall reviewing even a single page of material. Her breath shallows. It feels like her blood has stopped flowing to her brain. Her sight becomes blurry. Her eyes are wide open, but her spatial sense is confused. Her friends gather around and tease her, unaware and insensitive.

"Are you waiting for another perfect score, Song-yee?"

"I bet she is! Remember last time? She missed one question and cried!"

"You must've studied your butt off again."

The woman tries to keep her composure and barely answers, "No, I didn't study at all this time." She rests her head on her desk. The smell of the cheap wood makes everything more real. She muses about why she has not studied for the exam at all.

What got me here, so unprepared? This is so unlike her. She tries to think of all the possible reasons, none of which seem to make sense, and her stream of thoughts ends there.

When she's inside the dream, there's no way to know that this is only a dream—that she never needs to take another test in her real life, because she's well past that age. She graduated from school a long time ago and is now working full-time. She's an adult.

✳ ✳ ✳

Again, an abrupt scene transition. It is so seamless that she doesn't notice it. She's in class on a humid day before summer vacation. Her final day of exams.

Her desk is in the center of the classroom. On it lies an exam sheet full of questions, all unanswered.

I'm screwed! I can't remember a thing.

The woman is looking at the exam sheet, sweating. It doesn't help that she's wearing a heavy uniform, which traps the sweat, dripping from the inside. On top of that, murmurs passing among her classmates pierce her ears.

"Is this for real? This test is so easy!"

The woman starts to panic as the test turns into two pages, then three, and continues to grow. She flips to the next page and the next; she doesn't knows any answers.

The sounds of her peers turning the pages of their own exams fills the classroom. The woman has not solved a single problem yet.

The numbers in the math questions get muddled, and the big clock on the teacher's desk keeps on ticking hopelessly toward the finishing time. The ticktock rings loud and sharp, as if it's coming from inside her head.

Nervously, the woman jiggles her legs and bites her nails.

If I fail this test, my parents will be so disappointed!

The math teacher will summon me to the office after seeing my score.

What if they come to me during the break to cross-check the answers and see my wrong responses?

Nothing is more important for the woman right now than this test. The spikes of stress pierce her head as she starts to tear up. Then, the bright classroom suddenly plunges into shadow. Waves from the schoolyard flood in through the open windows, engulfing the classroom.

As her body is overtaken by the waves, the woman lets out a sigh of relief.

Thank God—the test will be canceled!

* * *

She woke up from her outrageous dream, her mind alert but blank. She felt disorientated and needed some time to get back to reality. Lying in bed, she repeated a series of affirmations.

I'm twenty-nine now. I graduated from high school a decade ago. I don't need to take midterms and finals and will never need to again.

Slowly, these self-assurances helped her senses to recover.

This was not her first time dreaming about exams. She was an ace student growing up, but her school life had been full of pressure around tests.

I'm so sick of this, she thought with a sigh.

* * *

Since this morning, dozens of infuriated customers demanding a refund have swarmed the Dallergut Dream Department Store. "How dare you sell this garbage?" they complain. Dallergut asked all employees to direct refund customers to his office. Since then, he hasn't come out.

Penny tries to estimate how many customers she's sent to his office so far. Dallergut pokes his head out and says, "Welcome," inviting them in and then closing the door.

Soon, his small office won't have room for any more customers. Penny thinks the logjam will only worsen the situation, creating complaints they never thought they'd have to deal with.

"Weather, I'm going to stop by Dallergut's office real quick."

Weather gives a big yawn instead of an answer. Penny takes it as: *Do what you want.*

She knocks on Dallergut's office door, holding a tray full of Calm Cookies, Dallergut's favorites.

"Excuse me. Can I come in?"

No sound from the inside. Penny puts her ear to the door. Strangely quiet. *Are all of them in meditation or something, holding hands side by side?* She hesitates a bit before turning the doorknob.

The office is empty.

Instead, the boxes once towering beside Dallergut's cabinet are now strewn across the floor. With the pile gone, a small, half-open door has been revealed, barely big enough for one person to squeeze through. Penny had no idea there was a hidden room inside the office.

She peeks through the door and sees a flight of blueish stone steps. The opening is narrow, but clean and comfortable enough for people to walk down. Penny hears murmurs drifting up the stairs.

"Dallergut? Are you there?" Penny's voice echoes down the stone steps.

"Penny, is that you? Oh, you came at just the perfect time!" She hears Dallergut but he's nowhere in sight. "There's a bundle of purchase confirmation letters on my desk. Can you bring them down here?"

"Purchase confirmation letters? I'm on it!" Penny puts down the cookie tray and starts looking for the letters. On the long desk are various certificates of quality signed by dreammakers, and other documents, including a thank you letter for a fifty-year contract renewal. Dallergut may dress neatly, but his desk is a mess. *The second-floor staff would have a field day cleaning this place*, Penny thinks, chuckling.

Penny goes through the documents as she whirls around the desk, tripping over the boxes at her feet. She makes a firm note to herself to ask Dallergut for permission to throw all these boxes away. There are dates written on top of each box; some are at least a decade old.

She finds the bundle of purchase confirmation letters hidden under a thick book.

"Dallergut! I found it! I'm coming down!"

Penny cautiously steps downstairs, with the cookie tray in one hand and the paper bundle in the other. The stairwell gets darker as she descends, but when she reaches the bottom, the space is brighter than the lobby.

Sitting around a marble round table are the customers, having tea with Dallergut.

Apart from the few still huffing and puffing, most seem to have softened from the tea Dallergut offered them. The astute Dallergut must've put drops of Relief or Relax syrup into the tea beforehand, Penny realizes.

As well as the lighting fixtures on the wall illuminating each corner, lamps outside the fake window create an illusion of sunrays streaming in.

"Are these the ones?" Penny hands him the pile.

"Yes. Thanks!"

"I had no idea you have a place like this."

"I created it for just this sort of situation. You don't want to make a scene that disturbs other customers' shopping experiences." Dallergut drops his voice to a mutter.

The customers had gone quiet when Penny's entered, but now were back to grumbling.

"So, what is it that you want to show us? Don't try to get away with any lame excuse," a female customer states, folding her arms.

"Do you have any idea how many of us have dreamed of being reenlisted? Why on earth would you sell a dream like that?" a guy sitting across from Dallergut snaps, putting his teacup on the table with a thud. Other people quickly follow suit.

"As I said, I was discharged last month, and I just

dreamed of returning to the military. Can you even imagine what that feels like?"

"Same with the exam dream! Is this some appalling sadistic hobby of yours? Tormenting people who are asleep?"

"I second that! I've been a longtime regular of your store, but I should boycott you from now on. Do you know that other up-and-coming stores sell feel-good dreams only? You need to keep up with the times if you want to keep your customers!" scoffs a woman wearing checked pajamas and sitting cross-legged.

Penny stands there at a loss, overwhelmed by the grim situation. It is her first time seeing customers being this aggressive toward Dallergut. But her boss seems entirely peaceful, as always.

"My dear customers, we thoroughly informed you what each product entailed when we sold it to you. Of course, we understand you wouldn't be here if you remembered that. We're sorry to hear you have no memory of it. But that's the way things go around here so we have to accept it."

"Right, we don't remember at all. Of course we don't! Why would anyone buy nightmares on purpose? That is nonsense!"

"Oh, my dear customer, I'm afraid these are technically different from typical nightmares. While we do sell a few involving ghosts or monsters, they are mainly for special holidays. What you purchased is not any nightmare. The exact title of this product is 'Overcoming Trauma.' Your dream was made by a young and very talented dreammaker who took time to fine-tune his craft. It's a very well-made dream," Dallergut affirms with pride.

Another round of murmurs from the customers. Some are asking each other, "What on earth is he talking about?" and others are muttering, "I think he's making things up." Not even Penny understands Dallergut's words.

"Anyway, it doesn't matter what it is. It's very unpleasant to face the memories we don't want to face, much less trauma. I want a full refund!" A man wearing the rented nightgown springs to his feet.

"Sir, as you know, we have a deferred payment system, so you actually haven't paid anything yet..." Penny chimes in.

Dallergut stops her. "It's okay, Penny. No need to stir up an argument." He turns back to the customers. "We've brought the purchase confirmation letters you signed when you bought the products. Please take a look. You'll recognize your signatures." Dallergut hands out the letters to each customer, then goes back to his seat. Penny glances at the letter of the customer next to her.

Purchase Confirmation Letter

This product titled "Overcoming Trauma" is a sale on commission. We have robust and strict guidelines from the association to handpick dreams with verified quality, creativity and effectiveness.

First, this dream was created for those who wish to train their minds and increase their self-esteem semipermanently. Its substance may vary depending on the purchaser's specific trauma.

Second, this product will only be paid for in full once the purchaser experiences positive emotions after waking up from the respective dream. At this point, its contract will be completed.

Third, given the traits of this dream, the purchaser may request an exchange or cancel the purchase within thirty days of the purchase date. However, it is not recommended, as the purchaser will not remember and will repurchase it anyway.

Last, the purchaser has been informed about the product details. Until the purchaser overcomes the trauma, they agree to dream it regularly, per the seller's advice.

(Signature)

*Note: After purchase, if the purchaser's daily life is affected by heavy stress or insomnia due to anxiety, the seller may cancel the sale at their discretion.

The signatures at the bottom do indeed belong to the customers themselves. Customers who were throwing temper tantrums moments ago now seem dumbfounded. The customers read and reread their letters, trying to process all the information.

"But how would this thing train our minds or increase our self-esteem? It's only increased my stress so far," asks one customer, who seems to be the first to understand the letter.

Penny agrees with this customer. This is the question that has been on her mind. She fully empathizes with everyone's frustrations.

"We sincerely apologize if our products have caused you stress. Of course, we can help you cancel your purchase if you wish never to dream it again. No payment has been processed, since you've not experienced positive results. So, no need to worry about refunds, either." As Dallergut says this, the customers start to thaw.

"Yes, we can accommodate whatever you wish to do. But how about we give it some time until you start to see results?" Penny carefully adds, seeing they're no longer in a cranky mood to argue.

"Do you know how awful it feels to relive the worst moment of your life? I want good things to live in my dreams." A customer shudders.

Dallergut consoles her. "But is it really the worst moment of your life?" he asks.

The customers all look at Dallergut. Their expressions all seem to say, *Let's see what nonsense this guy will come up with this time.*

"If you put it into perspective, the worst moments of your life were also when you had to persevere. Now that you've made it through the other side, it all depends on your perspective. Isn't it a testament to your strength, having endured those challenging times and prevailed?"

The customers muse over his words as they sip their tea. Penny takes the chance to hand out the Calm Cookies. Soon, only the sounds of cookies crunching and teacups clanging fill the underground room.

"Come to think of it, all psychotherapy starts from accepting your mind as it is. He does have a point," says the female customer in the checked pajamas. A few others nod in agreement.

After a while, exactly half of them ask to cancel the purchase.

"I understand. If you feel this way, we can proceed to withdraw your contract."

"I feel bad. I know I signed it myself. But I'd like to leave my trauma in the past."

"No worries at all. If you do have any change of heart, please come back anytime."

The customers who have opted to cancel the purchase rush out of the place, eager to get back to sleep. The other half, those who have decided to keep the contract, comfort each other, seeming resolved.

"Let's keep it up, everyone. No more army dreams next year!"

"Definitely. I really want to graduate from these test dreams, too. So, you're saying if I feel positive emotions after the dream, I should be good to go?"

"That's right—and I understand it won't be easy," Dallergut responds, standing up. "But please remember—you all are stronger than you think. You have achieved and overcome more than you realize. Once you accept that, things will get much better. This is my small gift to you for your decision to continue your resolution." Dallergut takes out a bottle of perfume the size of his palm and sprays it on the customers' pajama sleeves. A subtle summer forest scent spreads through their clothes.

"What is this?" asks the female customer in the checked pajamas, sniffing her sleeves. "It smells amazing."

"This perfume helps you sort through your thoughts in a positive direction. It won't have a drastic impact, but you'll find it useful. I use it myself sometimes. Please stop by anytime you feel frustrated. I can spray as much of this perfume as you need. And of course, you can also come back to cancel your contract, as the others did."

The customers return to the first floor, while Dallergut and Penny stay behind to clean up the teacups.

"Dallergut, what if every single one of them cancels it? The damage will be huge. Not only for us, but also for the dreammaker."

"We shall hope that won't happen."

"What? Are you saying there is no backup plan?"

"It is an incredible feat that half of those customers decided to keep the contract. I have no doubt this dream will have successful results for them," says Dallergut, glowing confidently.

* * *

The man continued to dream about being reenlisted in the army. It did leave him in a funk every time, but he soon realized he didn't need to be affected by anything as trifling as a dream. At the end of the day, he remained fully discharged from the military.

So the next time he had this dream, he laughed it off. *I survived the military, after all; what is there I can't do?*

The man recollected the day of his discharge—awkwardly stepping out into the world with his resolutions. And it didn't take long for him to realize that, having overcome the dream, his trauma was no longer a trauma, but a mark of his achievement.

✳ ✳ ✳

That is when the man's payment comes through to the Dallergut Dream Department Store. He doesn't dream about the military ever again.

✳ ✳ ✳

When the woman kept dreaming about taking tests, despite never having to take another one in real life, she finally acknowledged that she never fully got over the pressure from that period of her life.

She also realized how hard she's been on herself by assigning deadlines to everything—not only at work, but also with milestones like marriage and pregnancy: things that did not require a timeline, or even fulfillment.

One rainy morning, after having had the same test dream three nights in a row, she was determined to no longer be at the mercy of her own subconscious. She sat comfortably by the window, gazing out at the rain. She closed her eyes to focus on the feeling she'd had when she did well on her tests instead of the pressure she'd felt during exams.

I'm proud of myself for all the achievements I've made so far. I did a great job in the past and will do well at whatever I set my mind to. The self-encouragement was what she needed to let go. She extended kindness to herself.

Her test dreams no longer haunted her. And as time passed, she forgot entirely that she had ever had the dreams. That was when her payment came through to the Dallergut Dream Department Store.

★ ★ ★

Ding Dong. *"A large amount of Confidence has been paid for 'Overcoming Trauma.'"*

Ding Dong. *"A large amount of Self-Esteem has been paid for 'Overcoming Trauma.'"*

"The payments are coming through, finally." Dallergut checks the notifications on the monitor, delighted. "By the way, Penny, I'm heading to Maxim to deliver his share; do you want to come along? We don't have many customers today, so Weather should be able to cover it. Right, Weather?"

"If you can pick up some cream puffs on the way back, why not?" Weather adds.

"What do you say, Penny? Maxim is a people person. He just doesn't like to be outside. But he will love our company."

"Well… Okay," Penny reluctantly agrees.

On their way to meet Maxim, Penny can't help but worry. She intentionally slows her pace, trying to delay the meeting. She has heard so much about him. All the scary rumors may not be true, but she knows at least one of them is: that Maxim makes hair-raising dreams all day behind a blackout curtain in his back-alley production studio.

The "Overcoming Trauma" incident has shown her that Maxim's dreams are not always dark, but Penny still finds the idea of being around someone like him a little uncomfortable.

"Hurry up, Penny." Dallergut stops and turns back, far ahead of her.

"Yes, Dallergut. I'm coming!" Penny gives in and picks up the pace.

✶ ✶ ✶

Maxim's studio is like a quiet island isolated from the surrounding stores. Piles of leaves and old junk are scattered around the entrance. A vast window, covered by a blackout curtain, renders the studio dark and gloomy.

Dallergut gently knocks on the door. "Hey, Maxim, are you there?"

Unexpectedly, it's a polite, ordinary-looking young man who comes out. "Oh, hello, Dallergut! What brings you to this humble abode?" In a short-sleeved shirt and ripped jeans under a black work apron, Maxim is tall and slender in physique, with broad shoulders and long arms and legs. He stands with a natural slouch. Watching his unstable steps as he guides them in, Penny is clouded by a scary thought that perhaps his spine was once completely fractured and has just been reattached.

The three sit around Maxim's worktable, which he hastily cleans in front of them. Dallergut enjoys the wine-pickled figs that Maxim offers. As for Penny, the crimson figs look rather frightening, like blood, possibly due to the dark studio lighting—or her own mood—and she doesn't dare try one.

"Excuse me, could we possibly turn up the light? Or how about we open the blackout curtains? It's just a bit too dark and the sunlight is beautiful today," Penny suggests, partially because the darkness scares her and partially because she wants a better view of Maxim's studio.

"I'm sorry, but my dreams will turn blurry if they're exposed to too much light. They need to be sharper and more vivid than other dreams. The whole point is lost if people find out they're dreaming, you know? I hope you understand."

"That makes total sense." Penny realizes her request was disrespectful, and tries to make up for it by embracing his hospitality. She puts a fig pickle inside her mouth. To her surprise, the fruit is sweet and soft.

"Here are your payments." Dallergut pulls out a thick envelope from his inside pocket.

"Oh, they came through faster than expected. These customers are resilient. I bet it's all your doing, right, Dallergut?"

"Of course not. It's all thanks to our strong and wise customers who recognize your dreams' true potential."

"Thank you for doing business with me. I never thought people would like my unpleasant dreams at all."

"No, thank *you*! I appreciate you standing your ground in creating these dreams. I truly believe the world needs the dreams you make."

It looks like Maxim's getting emotional. He stares upward with his lips pursed, as if trying to fight back tears, but Penny can't be sure in the dark lighting.

"That's very flattering to hear. But you know, this business can make you doubt yourself. Everyone has dark moments they don't like to remember. And maybe that can be an option, you know, to put all that behind you. It may even be the best option. So, I sometimes get wound up, thinking what I'm doing is meaningless... All these thoughts haunt me sometimes," Maxim says.

Dallergut is lost in thought. He seems to choose his words carefully.

Maxim isn't as intimidating as Penny anticipated, so she doesn't mind interrupting. "Then why not just be straightforward? You can make dreams that show people's happiest moments or achievements," she suggests.

"You certainly know how to lighten the mood." Maxim seems to like Penny's idea.

"It'll make everyone happy, for sure!" she says. "Way easier to receive payments, too!"

"You're looking out for me, aren't you?" For a moment, Penny's concerned he might have taken her response the wrong way, that she was implying something about his finances. But then it dawns on her he's joking.

"Penny, do you know what sets a good dream apart from an ordinary one?" Dallergut asks.

"Well, I'm sure you've told me before…" Penny tries to recall the many nuggets of wisdom Dallergut has shared. Maxim watches her ponder.

"You said the value of a dream depends on the customer…" she murmurs. "Oh, that's right! The difference between a good dream and an ordinary dream depends on whether the customers find enlightenment. The point is that they need to discover the lessons themselves rather than us spoon-feeding them. That's what makes a dream good."

"That's right. Overcoming hardships in the past makes people who they are now: survivors and heroes. Our job is to make them realize that on their own."

"Yes, that is why we sell dreams. At the end of the day, it's all up to the customer. Am I right?" Penny says.

"Dallergut, you certainly have a great employee working with you," Maxim says, smiling as brightly as the sunlight outside.

FIVE
THE DREAMMAKERS' GENERAL ASSEMBLY

Today, the Dallergut Dream Department Store is relatively quiet. Customers are calmly shopping, and Dallergut is roaming around the lobby with a snack basket under his arm, handing out Deep Sleep Candy to those leaving empty-handed.

"Can I have one more?" says a female customer in a golden lace nightdress, teasingly sticking out her hand.

"Do you have a day off tomorrow?"

"No, I have work, yet again."

"Then take one only. Two will make you sleep through your alarm."

The customer looks glum as she leaves the store, her shoulders stooped at the thought of going to work tomorrow.

It's a relaxing workday for Penny. She idly fills her time wiping and rewiping the same Eyelid Scales, and by the time her shift is almost over, she is just sitting at the front desk with a blank stare. Next to her, Weather keeps filling her memo pad with something and then erasing it, only to repeat the same thing all over again.

The pendulum clock in the lobby says 5:30 p.m.

"Weather, can you start getting ready? I reserved a taxi for 6:00 p.m., and it'll be here anytime." Dallergut approaches the front desk, his snack basket now empty.

"Oh my, is it time already? I still haven't decided on the Christmas decorations yet. I was planning to order them today…" Weather seems impatient, unable to sit still.

"Are you two heading somewhere? And what about the Christmas decorations? Christmas is still months away," Penny asks, confused.

"You'd be surprised! There's only one decoration store on this street. If you're late to the ordering game, you'll be stuck with leftover items. Last year, I had to buy a muddy tree that looked like it was sloppily chopped down for as much as 100 gordens. I still remember whenever Motail passed by that tree, he'd tease that I had decorated a fire log," Weather mumbles, her eyes glued to the memo pad.

"So, where are you two heading that requires a cab reservation?"

Hastily, Weather picks up a piece of crumpled paper from the front desk and hands it to Penny. Penny smooths out the paper and starts reading.

Dear all dreammakers and sellers,

This year's general assembly will take place at Nicholas's house, located in the entryway to the Million-Year Snow Mountain on the north side. This year's agenda is "How to tackle the rising number of 'no-shows.'" We sincerely ask that all members attend.

Best regards,

Nicholas, President of the Dream Industry Staff Association

"Dallergut is invited, and he can take one person to accompany him. It's a great opportunity to meet famous dreammakers in person. As for me, though, I've grown a bit tired of it…" Weather says indifferently.

"How about Vigo Myers? He loves dreams so much, I'm sure he would love to meet the dreammakers," says Penny.

"Not necessarily. Yes, Myers loves dreams, but he has…rather complex feelings about the dreammakers." Weather lowers her voice. "He has a bit of a jealousy issue. He was expelled just days before his college graduation, for some reason. He could have become a promising dreammaker had he graduated. And apparently he still holds a grudge. So it's best not to mention the word *dreammaker* around him."

Weather returns to her memo pad, scribbling down "Christmas signature garland x 30 m," "satin ribbon x 30 rolls," "cotton wools x 1,000" and "fake antlers x 3."

"If you're busy, Weather, I can go by myself," Dallergut says stiffly.

"You sure?" Weather does not hide her delight.

"Of course. I'll just shove food into my mouth and stand awkwardly by myself in a room full of dreammakers. I'll be totally fine."

Weather's smile fades.

"Can I come?" Penny chimes in. "I don't have any plans after work today." She means it. She's not trying to be nice; she's genuinely interested in attending.

"Would you?" Weather says, beaming along with Dallergut.

"I'll just get my coat. Give me a second!" Dallergut says.

Weather now seems more at ease. Humming an old carol, she adds "Christmas tree lights" to her list.

"I had no idea decorating for Christmas was part of our front desk job," Penny says, making a mental note to pick up some tips from Weather so she can prepare for next year's season in advance.

"Nah, it's for whoever likes to do it. And I like this type of work. When I first got pregnant with my youngest child, I lost myself in a shopping spree to decorate the baby's room, and when I came to, I was already in my last month! Come to think of it, this was Myers's job before it became mine."

"Manager Myers handled the Christmas decorations?"

"Just for a year. He would demand the staff align the branches in perfect symmetry, pick up stray ornaments if they fell, and so on. Driving everyone crazy. Of course, the ever-tidy second-floor staff members were thrilled... But for others, it was madness. So, for everyone's sake, I decided to take over, because I love shopping. Anyway, I want to make the order today so we receive all the packages in advance and can relax. It's an important priority of mine." Weather seems genuinely joyful.

Dallergut comes back out wearing a brown coat with blue rain boots that look entirely out of place.

"Umm, Dallergut. I think the shoes you were wearing before are much better..."

Just then, the taxi arrives with two short honks.

"Shall we get going?" says Dallergut, and they head out to the car.

"Hello, Mr. Dallergut. It's my honor to serve you today." A young taxi driver takes off his hat and extends his hand to Dallergut in the back seat.

"You're too kind! Thank you for making it in time."
Dallergut misses the extended hand, apparently distracted
by his boots, which seem too small for him. Looking
awkward, the driver raises the radio volume with his rejected hand and starts driving.

The taxi slowly moves through the downtown. Dallergut looks out of the window in silence. Penny feels
a bit hungry, having only had a small lunch. Her stomach growls, but fortunately, it's buried by the sound of
the radio.

"By the way, am I really allowed to join you? I assume
only VIPs get invited to the general assembly… Weather's a veteran staffer, but I'm just an unknown newbie."

"Don't worry. The general assembly used to be a
meeting for authorities to discuss and resolve important
issues in the dream industry. Nowadays, it's just a light
dinner gathering. Nobody cares who brings whom. It's
better this way. A light and casual setting allows for more
productive and open discussions."

"But I saw the official invitation. The agenda item is
urgent this time."

"Are you referring to the no-show issue?"

"Yes. I know what it means: customers who preorder
their dreams but fail to pick them up on time because
they don't fall asleep."

"Yes, you're right. It is indeed a crucial issue. The

damage is especially severe for those of us who use the pay-later system."

"Could it impact our business?" Penny worries that the job she worked so hard to land could be in jeopardy.

"It's not bad enough to affect our business. We've been dealing with this issue for as long as I can remember. Let's hope some great ideas emerge at the meeting today."

Through the car window, Penny notices Maxim's dull studio.

"Will Maxim be there as well?" she asks.

"I'm not sure. He usually spends all his time working on his dreams. He isn't a regular attendee at this kind of thing. Were you hoping to see him there?"

"Well... It would be nice to see a familiar face." Penny fiddles with a strand of her hair.

As they pass an alleyway, the streets empty out. Down a highway on the outskirts of the city the Million-Year Snow Mountain comes into view, bright and blindingly white.

"I'm afraid you'll have to walk the rest of the way. Cars can't enter here," says the driver, speaking for the first time after the long, silent drive.

The road to Nicholas's cabin is unsuitable for Penny's short ankle boots. Her legs keep sinking deep into the snow. Meanwhile, Dallergut's walking ahead in his rain boots, oblivious to Penny's struggles.

"There it is. That's Nicholas's cabin." Dallergut stops.

Passing several trees as big as houses, the cabin—which is more like a mansion—rises out of nowhere. Its little silver decorations sparkle more than the snow surrounding it.

"How come we don't see this from our village?"

"It's not visible in the sun; the house is whiter than the snow. This view never gets old!"

"But it can't be easy to venture outside if you live here."

"Perfect for the guy. He just stays at home except during the winter."

Penny scowls. Her socks are soaking from the wet snow. When they reach the cabin, an old man who looks at least twenty years older than Dallergut throws open the door and jumps out.

"Dallergut!" the old man excitedly greets him and grabs him by the hand. His short hair and eyebrows are as silver as the snow.

"Nicholas! How have you been?" Dallergut eagerly returns the handshake.

"You're first to arrive again! These dreammakers, they hate it when their customers are late, but look at them…" Nicholas clucks with disapproval. "Is this your new staffer? Filling in for Weather, I presume."

"Yes. This is Penny. Penny, meet Nicholas, the host and the owner of the house."

"Hello, I'm Penny. I started working at the Dallergut dream store earlier this year."

"Nice to meet you, Penny. I assume you've heard about me."

Penny has not heard about Nicholas. When she saw the invitation, she just assumed he was one of the association staff members. She meets his eyes with an awkward smile, trying to hide her *I-don't-know-anything-about-you* face.

"Hurry up and come on in before your feet get frostbite from those damp socks!"

Penny hesitantly glances at Dallergut before taking off her wet socks. She awkwardly puts her boots back on with the backs folded down and steps inside.

"Please wait here. I'll get you some food. The ribs today have been grilled perfectly in my brand-new high-quality oven. I've also got plenty of liquor to go with them."

Nicholas leads them to the dining room. Behind a long dining table, a giant arched window gives way to a frosty snow-covered landscape. Perennial plants on the table are decorated with fairy lights, and a sizable pine tree towers over the kitchen. It all seems strangely fitting.

Penny thinks this place could be great for Christmas decoration inspiration. If only Weather were here. She wishes she could take pictures.

"Dallergut, what dreams does the host make? I've never heard of a dreammaker named Nicholas."

"Oh, I see. Yes, his real name might not sound familiar. Do you want to take a guess, having looked around this place?"

"I'd imagine he creates fairy-tale-like dreams. An old grandpa in the Million-Year Snow Mountain… Inside a cabin full of glittering decorations… And a feast… This place feels like Christmas!"

"So you've caught on!"

"I'm sorry?"

"You can't talk about Christmas without Nicholas, and vice versa. They're inextricable."

Dallergut stares at Penny as if to say, *How many more hints do you need? I basically told you everything.*

Thanks to that, Penny gets it. "Is he Santa Claus?"

"Yes, he is. But we usually call him Nicholas here."

Santa Claus is a famous dreammaker whose skills are on par with the Legendary Big Five—Yasnoozz Otra, Kick Slumber, Wawa Sleepland, Doje and Babynap Rockabye. But he's only known to sell his dreams at Christmas. He insists on working exclusively in the winter.

That he can still live in such luxury while working only during the Christmas season is a testament to his enormous talent.

"Nicholas has no desire for fame. He is just a simple old man who loves the Christmas season and kids. Oh, and this, too." Dallergut holds up a fancy-looking silver fork and smiles.

Penny thinks Nicholas has the perfect work-life balance. A life worth aspiring to.

After much rattling in the kitchen, Nicholas comes out with a bread basket and fruit salad. Penny admires his silver hair and matching silver beard. She and Dallergut help him set the table.

* * *

By the time the places are set, other guests have started to assemble. The first to arrive after Penny and Dallergut is Babynap Rockabye, the precognitive dreammaker. Maxim is right behind her. Rockabye seems to have chosen him over her usual entourage for today.

Both of them come in with their shoes soaking wet from the snow. Maxim's big build juxtaposed with Rockabye's tiny physique makes for a striking contrast. Strangely, though, they exude a similar energy.

Do all these veteran dreammakers share the same unique aura? Penny remembers feeling this same aura from Dallergut when she first met him. It dawns on her how thrilling it is to be among these incredible dreammakers.

It makes her feel like she's one of them. She could get used to occasions like this.

"Hello!" Penny greets Rockabye in an unusually excited tone.

Surprisingly, Rockabye remembers her. "Oh, a new face in place of Weather this time! You're that adorable lady I saw at the dream store when I brought my last batch."

"Penny, so good to see you here," Maxim greets her, almost teary with excitement, much to Penny's surprise. Could he really be that elated to see her? She knows that can't be true.

Tears are now running down Maxim's face. "Oh, this is just because Nicholas's house is too bright for my eyes. By the way, Penny, after you visited my studio, I changed the black curtains to gray. You pointed out how dark it was…"

"To…gray?"

"Yes. The gray color transmits more sunlight than the black—by three percent."

"Oh…" Penny doesn't know what to say, so she just looks back at Maxim, who's standing there like an overgrown kid, waiting for a compliment, although the bright light warps his features.

"Why don't you put on some shades, kiddo?" Nicholas taps Maxim on the shoulder, offering him a pair of sunglasses. "And stop making gloomy dreams, would you? Live a merry life, you're still young."

Maxim seamlessly takes the sunglasses from Nicholas, as if this isn't the first time he has worn them. "So many people are oblivious to how dangerous the world is. Warm blankets, warm meals like this and a safe home... They don't last. I want to prepare people to be strong for the world," Maxim says solemnly, putting on the over-size aviator sunglasses.

"It amazes me how you worry so much over every little thing, because you don't look the type. It's all in your head, kiddo. As far as I know, the world has seen scarier things. Jealousy, inferiority complexes... These are the things to watch out for nowadays, scarier than a wild beast chasing you."

"That's actually a good business idea!" Maxim seems interested.

"Sorry to interrupt, but why don't we save business talk for later? Please take a seat." Dallergut intervenes and sets the tone.

Rockabye sits right next to Nicholas. Maxim, whom Penny had guessed would sit next to Rockabye, hesitates, then sits beside Penny. Penny fights the urge to read too much into it, but it's hard to discern his intentions behind the sunglasses.

With everything made from fresh ingredients, Nicholas's feast is spectacular, even with minimum seasonings. Rockabye is on her second plate of fruit salad.

"This is amazing! Nothing is better than fresh fruit."

Penny has been waiting for everybody else to arrive before she starts her meal, but when the freshly grilled back ribs are served, waiting becomes excruciating.

"Please go ahead and start," says Nicholas. "It's no good when the food turns cold. You can have as much as you want. As we speak, I have another round of food baking in the oven for our latecomers."

At this, Penny aims her fork at a piece of meat and dips it into the gravy. Just as she is about to put it into her mouth, two new faces appear before her that immediately stop her in her tracks.

Technically, they are familiar faces to Penny, but this is her first time seeing them in person.

Standing before her is a fair-skinned lady with long, beautiful auburn hair. Accompanying her is a middle-aged woman with a short, asymmetric bob, wearing a long, fashionable coat that comes down to her ankles.

"Wawa Sleepland *and* Yasnoozz Otra are standing in front of me? Unbelievable!" Penny makes a great fuss, unable to hide her excitement.

"You're here early, Dallergut. And I can see you're not with Weather today," says Wawa Sleepland, giving Penny a nod.

"Oh my God, I've been a huge fan of yours since I was little! Well, not little, but since my school days, which makes sense, because it's been less than ten years since your debut, right?" Penny is talking gibberish, mesmerized by Sleepland's beauty.

"Long time no see, Wawa. You look well. And Yasnoozz, you look terrific, too." Dallergut greets them with such ease, like it's just another day.

"Dallergut, did you know my lifelong dream is to have one of their dreams!" Penny exclaims.

Across from Penny sit Wawa Sleepland, Yasnoozz Otra and Babynap Rockabye, all side by side, tasting the back ribs. Penny can barely eat her dish, too busy glancing at them. She doesn't notice Maxim carefully rotating the back rib platter so that the soft part of the meat faces her.

"Penny, whose dream would you want to have the most?" Dallergut quietly asks.

"For me… It would have to be Sleepland's."

"Ah, Wawa Sleepland, wonderful choice! She makes such scenic dreams. I've dreamed one of hers before, and it was incredible. I didn't want to wake up from it. It was set in the Middle Ages, and I was overlooking a city from a fortress in the rain. The sky was twinkling above me, the moon and the stars coming closer the more I reached to touch them." Dallergut seems lost in thought, his eyes distant.

"I assume they must be costly?"

"Of course. But Yasnoozz's are even more expensive than Wawa's." Dallergut points his shoulder at Yasnoozz Otra, who is sipping wine and making small talk with Babynap Rockabye.

"I've heard Yasnoozz Otra's dreams are priceless. A lot of her dreams are about putting ourselves in others' shoes, aren't they? Is there a particular dream that especially costs more?"

"The longer the dreams are, the pricier."

"By much?"

"By as much as it costs to have an opportunity to live another person's life."

"Is that even possible?" Penny's eyebrows go up.

"Everything is possible in a dream. You work in the business; don't you know that by now?" Dallergut gently smiles.

"Hey, you, Dallergut! I was meaning to stop by your store," says Yasnoozz Otra from across the table as she reaches for the pepper shaker.

"Oh, what did you need? I can have my staff take care of it for you. You're a very busy person all year round."

"It's fine. Yes, I'm busy, but I do enjoy some time off, too, you know. I only make a couple of dreams a year, anyway. It's just that they're all too long… Speaking of which, will my products be up at your store soon?"

"I'm sorry, but your price is a bit over our budget… You always require advance payments," Dallergut says.

"Of course. Gorgeous coats like that one won't just sit there waiting for me to make enough money to buy them. They'd be long gone." Otra glances at the long coat hanging on the coat stand in the corner and brushes the glittering crystal brooch on her blouse with her hand. "Can you at least consider selling my new short-length dreams next season? That should be a happy medium."

"I'd be honored."

Otra winks at Dallergut as she sprinkles pepper all over her plate. After filling her glass with the extravagant wine that Nicholas offered, she seems satisfied.

Nicholas is counting the number of outstanding guests who have yet to arrive. "Is Bancho bailing out? He's such a workaholic. Must be working on something worth more than a little coin. Or he has got so carried away feeding wild animals that he lost track of time—"

Bark, bark, bark!

Nicholas is interrupted by the barking sound.

"Hello, guys! Sorry I'm late!" shouts Bancho.

"Speak of the devil," Nicholas clucks.

A young man walks in carrying wet shoes, followed by dogs as big as wolves, sniffing his wet socks. "Winter comes so fast in the mountains. It's already freezing, so

I got delayed trying to prepare. I had to get the fire logs and fix the beds for this gang, you know."

The unpretentious man takes off his washed-out quilted jacket, hangs it on the coat stand and grabs a seat.

"Animora, come over here by the fireplace, or you'll catch a cold," Dallergut offers thoughtfully.

Penny's taking in the gathering of the dreammakers. It's a once-in-a-lifetime moment. Her eyes meet Bancho's. She tries to laugh away the awkwardness, but to her surprise, Bancho kindly introduces himself.

"Hi, happy to meet you! You must be here with Dallergut. I always feel bad I'm not able to visit his store more often… It's just that I rarely leave the mountains—I'm busy taking care of a lot of animal friends. Oh, my name is Animora Bancho. I create dreams for animals. I believe they're on display at Dallergut's dream store on the fourth floor. I owe Mr. Speedo big time."

His jovial introduction sets Penny at ease.

"Hello, I'm Penny, I work at the dream store. We have many adorable furry customers, thanks to your dreams. We owe *you* big time!"

Few dream stores sell dreams for animals, as their emotions—while the animals do feel them—are not as dramatic as a human's. But Dallergut always buys Bancho's dreams in bulk. *Dallergut must have high regard for Bancho*, Penny thinks.

Bancho pays close attention to his dogs' growling, as if he is communicating with them. With a nod, he thanks Nicholas for the food, and slices the unseasoned part of the lean meat to hand out to the dogs first. He wipes his steak knife on his worn-out shirt, which is more or less a rag.

Nicholas clucks at the sight of him. "I know there's virtue in staying away from money, but you should at least try to maintain your dignity. Can you please get rid of those old clothes and buy yourself some new ones? How can you create good dreams when you're on a tight budget? Dreams are all about creating fantasies that don't exist in reality. Dream and fantasy always go hand in hand, you know. And you can't make fantasy dreams when you're strapped for cash," Nicholas admonishes.

"I'm fine. Everything I need is in the mountains, and these guys never leave me bored. I rarely spend money anywhere. It's been my dream to live a life like this."

Bancho seems to mean it. But he also looks rather shabby compared to all the other elegant and glamorous dreammakers.

Their chatter continues, but is interrupted by the clinking of glass. A swarm of glowing creatures are head-butting the window.

"Looks like they're here," Nicholas mutters as he

pushes open the kitchen window, and tiny silver-winged creatures flood in—the Leprechauns.

Instead of taking a seat, a dozen Leprechauns gather around the breadbasket in the center of the dining table with their wings folded.

"Nicholas, can you chop the food into bite-size pieces for us?" asks a chubby Leprechaun who looks like the leader, his voice like a clattering crystal bead. He's struggling with a piece of bread bigger than himself.

"How impudent, you little scamps. I told you not to call me by my name when I'm at work! Only my work name—Santa Claus. Remember?"

"But you only work at Christmas, Nicholas," chuckles Babynap Rockabye.

"I have to work twenty-four seven, all year round, to study every kid's tastes so that I can have their dreams ready before Christmas Day. Do you know how capricious they are? You think I lounge around in the mountains doing nothing?" Nicholas steams.

"Okay, Nicholas. Why don't we start our discussion now that everyone's here?" Dallergut asks.

"Kick Slumber isn't here yet. It might take a while before he arrives, given the rough road… Why don't we wait for him?" says Nicholas.

"Actually, he won't make it today," Wawa Sleepland

chimes in, elegantly spreading honey butter on her bread. "He's gone to Kamnik Cliffs for product research."

"That far? No wonder I couldn't get hold of him." Nicholas seems disappointed.

"Wawa, how do you know that?" Otra asks, genuinely curious.

"Well... His fans post his every move on the internet. I happened to see a picture of him there on social media," Wawa Sleepland says vaguely, her face turning red.

"By the way, I see Doje is not here again this year."

"Doje rarely comes out to events like these. He must be training again, somewhere far away," says Otra, opening a new bottle of wine.

"Now then, let's get started with our agenda," says Nicholas as he stands up. "Why don't we first discuss how big the loss was from no-shows last month."

"We lost fifteen percent of our projected profit. It was on our contract that we wouldn't be able to receive payments for the unsold dreams from no-shows," the leader of the Leprechauns says, munching on a piece of cheese. Five of them are all feasting on the same slice.

"In fact, most of you famous dreammakers can't relate to this. All the products on the first floor of the dream store sell out in a flash. We indie dreammakers are the ones that have to pay the price," grumbles a Leprechaun in a pink puffed blouse.

"That's nonsense! I have so many customers who don't take my conception dreams. Dallergut, tell these little ones what happened to that dream I had asked you to handle," Babynap Rockabye rebuts.

"So… There was a couple who didn't pick up their conception dream for two weeks," Dallergut says, pausing to refresh his memory. "We tried to send it to their friends or parents, but even they didn't show up. We ended up giving it to the wife's best friend's sister, who I imagine must've been puzzled because she hadn't seen the couple for a long time—plus she was single. But I had no choice. I was running against the deadline."

"But you're rich, Rockabye. The damage is insurmountable for poor dreammakers like us," the Leprechaun leader grunts, his golden watch sparkling on his wrist.

"I told you to do some marketing," Nicholas clucks. "We Santa Clauses have been spreading rumors since ages ago, one of which was: 'Santa won't have presents for kids who go to bed late.' Marketing is all about storytelling. Kids these days go head over heels for good stories. Slipping in presents when they're asleep…what a fantastic idea our ancestors came up with!" He shrugs his shoulders in pride.

"And thanks to that *rumor*, poor parents have been suffering the consequences, hustling to get presents in time for Christmas Day. And who made up the story about hanging stockings? Now everyone has to sleep with their stinky socks by the bedside!" Babynap Rockabye rebukes Nicholas. She seems especially sensitive when it comes to matters involving kids and parents.

"I mean, it's not technically a rumor. We do bring presents when they're asleep!" Nicholas says defensively. "It's just that our presents happen to be good dreams, not some transforming cars. And if you've ever taken those sleeping socks from the Noctilucas, you'd know how long the ankle is. It's roomy and you can hold on to them like a handle. It stretches really well, too..." Nicholas realizes he's rambling on and on. He quickly changes the subject. "Anyway! To get to the point: I would like to suggest having the sellers partially pay for the damages incurred from no-shows."

Suddenly, all eyes swivel to Dallergut, including Penny's.

"Nicholas, I don't think this is quite the right place to discuss this. I'm the only seller here," Dallergut counters calmly, with a steady gaze. "To discuss fines for the sellers, we'd need to gather all the sellers from the industry, and I can guarantee you the discussion will take all night. For tonight, shouldn't we instead try to find the root cause of the issue?" He pivots tactfully.

"I agree. It's excessive to ask the sellers to take responsibility for no-shows to reduce our dreammakers' damages," Wawa Sleepland defends Dallergut. "We need to continue our respected partnership between dreammakers and sellers, regardless of mere profit."

"Then what do you all think is the reason for no-shows? My business is seasonal, so I can't really suggest a reason myself," Nicholas says.

"It's not so simple. No-shows are intertwined with complex personal issues and national events," responds the smartest-looking Leprechaun. Penny thinks their voices are very loud for creatures with such a tiny build. But on closer examination, she notices they are each wearing a mini wireless microphone.

"It should be common knowledge to all of us that when customers struggle with personal issues, they don't come to pick up dreams until dawn."

Everyone nods in unison.

"And setting aside personal issues, let's say we have the World Cup in Europe. Oh, don't get me started with these World Cups. I mean, I hope everyone here has done at least a basic study on the customers," the Leprechaun says haughtily. "So, everyone in Asia will stay up all night to watch games happening in Europe, right? The issue is that these worldwide events are increasing, as are the number of live-streaming channels." The Leprechauns seem to be very knowledgeable.

"I see. Penny, I think a young lady like you might

have something to say to shed light on this?" Nicholas gives her the floor.

"In my opinion… The exams can also play a role." Penny manages to recall the no-show student customer whose dream product Motail snuck in. "There are many customers from Korea during my shifts… They all go through the same exam period at once. And when they do, they usually stay up all night. But this is not a long-term issue. They only stay up for a night or two before the exam. Apparently, cramming for exams is something that happens worldwide."

"That makes sense. How about you, Maxim?"

Maxim, suddenly thrust into the spotlight, is caught off guard. His words catch in his throat, and he has a coughing fit. When he finally manages to settle down, he speaks in a low, solemn tone. "In my case, I'm not really affected much. At least you all have customers preorder dreams. I don't have many customers to begin with, so…" He blushes. "The only stock I produce is for Dallergut, who buys it directly from me. So, I don't get enough preorders to have many no-shows in the first place."

"No wonder you were able to enjoy the food," Nicholas jokes, and everyone bursts into laughter. Penny sees Maxim's face go even more scarlet and is intrigued to catch this unexpected side of him.

"How about you, Bancho? Are there any damages on your end?" Babynap Rockabye asks with a worried look. Animora Bancho has not been eating his food, seeming preoccupied with feeding the dogs and slicing the bread and meat for the Leprechauns.

"Bancho is so sweet," Penny mutters. Maxim grabs the breadbasket and starts grinding the bread into smaller pieces too.

"No, I'm great. Animals sleep a lot by comparison. And there aren't many things they find worth trading their sleep for," Bancho says, his eyes fixated on the dogs lying flat by his feet. One with black scruff is sleeping peacefully, resting its head on Bancho's foot.

"That's right!" shouts the clever-looking Leprechaun, startling Penny. "Bancho is correct. There are so many entertaining things that keep people up all night." The clever Leprechaun flies around a plate. "Playing video games, scrolling through their smartphones, talking the night away with their partners... They put off sleep to enjoy the present!" The Leprechaun is now on Nicholas's shoulder, his wings folded. Nicholas is annoyed, but doesn't shoo him away.

"I agree," Otra adds. "They're a different kind from the ones pulling all-nighters to cram for their tests. The latter's no-show is temporary. What we need to worry about are the voluntary bedtime procrastinators."

The Leprechauns munch on the bread, satisfied to have the others' agreement.

"Maxim, why did you grind the bread into crumbs? You should have cut them into bite-size pieces. You know how things are done. What's wrong with you?" the Leprechaun in the puffy pink blouse rebukes Maxim, who turns red again.

"Well, then what can we do to make them go to sleep on time?" Nicholas contemplates. "Can we do something with your Sleep Candy, Dallergut?"

"Those candies only work on those already asleep." Dallergut shakes his head.

"What if we generate profits from other streams to make up for these no-show losses? We're more than happy to share our insights," the leader of the Leprechauns brags.

"Where would we generate those profits from?" Penny asks. She remembers her first tour of the Dallergut dream store, when Mogberry vented about how deceptive the Leprechauns could be. She'd said that the Leprechauns used dirty tricks to maximize dream payments.

"You've all been wondering how we were able to expand our business enough to move to the center of the main street." The leader walks to the middle of the table. "If you sell a 'Flying Dream' to a hundred customers, about sixty of them will submit dream payments. We usually get Freedom or Wonder as payment. But we also get Regret and Loss, because when you wake up in reality, you realize you can't actually fly. As you all know, these negative emotions don't convert to good money. So we came up with an idea!" The leader steps aside to give the smart Leprechaun room to speak.

"From our internal research," the clever Leprechaun says, "we have found that paralysis dreams are more profitable than flying dreams. The kinds of dreams that make you feel incapacitated, where your feet feel heavy like steel when you're trying to run forward, or your body feels sluggish when you're trying to fight back against a bully... When our customers have such dreams, we receive way more payments of Freedom. They feel liberated when they wake up from those dreams and are able to move again!" He pulls out a calculator and taps the buttons. "As you can see here, the results show way more profits. This will easily offset the no-show losses." The clever Leprechaun proudly shows off his calculations, but they're met with a lukewarm reaction.

"You guys are not getting this... There's a reason why our business is thriving," he continues. "Hey Maxim! How about we collaborate with you on your nightmares? If we team up and make a dream of being chased by scary thugs, but your legs don't move, it could be our biggest hit ever! You're in a chase the whole dream, and it ends right when you're about to get caught. I already hear the payments coming in," the Leprechaun coaxes Maxim from a perch on his broad shoulder.

"I don't play such silly games with my customers!" Maxim picks up the Leprechaun with his fingers and puts him down on the table.

"Ha ha, Mogberry was right about you guys." Dallergut gives a cold smirk. "I heard a rumor that the Leprechauns were fooling around, putting the wrong labels on their dreams. So, that was true. How dare you trick us into this and meddle with our customers?" He doesn't raise his voice at all, just calmly admonishes them, but he's clearly furious.

"I-I'm sorry." The leader apologizes, seeming to sense the gravity of the situation.

"If I ever catch you doing such sneaky things again, your contract will be canceled," Dallergut warns the Leprechauns.

"Dallergut is right. We all know this kind of trick can work, but there's a reason none of us use it as you did," Otra says as she takes a last gulp of her wine and puts the glass down. "Now, let's not distract ourselves with all this unhelpful talk. Why don't we start wrapping things up and get to a solution? I know everyone's busy. What's your conclusion, Dallergut?"

Dallergut straightens his collar and clears his throat. "First of all, please don't be offended by what I'm about to say. I'm just an old seller offering a straightforward and simple view."

"Eh, you always have such a long preface," Nicholas says to him.

"I believe we already *have* reached a conclusion. As Bancho and the Leprechauns mentioned, people put off going to bed because they have things to do that they think are more fun than sleeping. How about we twist this perspective?" Dallergut chuckles, as if it is such an easy and obvious fix.

The Leprechauns are giving Dallergut their full attention, sitting upright.

"The solution is to make dreams even more entertaining than the things keeping people awake. I believe you dreammakers all have the talent to make it possible."

After a beat of silence, the room breaks into bright laughter.

"So you're saying, at the end of the day, it's all because our dreams aren't entertaining enough? You got us, Dallergut." Nicholas gives a hearty laugh.

"I didn't say it in that manner, but if you must put it that way, I'll have to admit you're right," Dallergut responds sociably.

The Leprechauns clap among themselves in agreement.

"On that note, I think this wraps up our discussion. Shall we raise our glasses and enjoy the rest of our dinner?" Otra holds up her newly refilled glass.

"Good idea!"

Everyone else raises their glasses.

Nicholas stands up and shouts, "Let's eat well, sleep well and have sweet dreams!"

SIX

BESTSELLER OF THE MONTH

It's the last week of December. The streets glow like a fantasyland. Thanks to Weather's speedy arrangement of the Christmas decorations, the Dallergut Dream Department Store is decorated more splendidly than ever. The displays, from the first floor to the fifth, are wrapped with Christmas lights, sparkling like jewelry boxes. Weather originally proposed changing to more glittery wrapping paper, but the second-floor staff and manager rejected the idea.

"Do you have any idea how much glitter falls off from those sparkly wrappers? It requires so much cleanup."

The Noctilucas also try out a different, seasonal style for the nightdresses they lend out, embroidering them with snowflake patterns. But the customers don't seem to like it.

"Don't you have pretty pajamas? This is ugly," one kid says, pouting.

"If you don't want to wear this, kid, wear warm clothes to sleep. And try not to kick your blanket in your sleep," one Noctiluca scolds as it straightens up the kid's clothes with its thick paws.

The Christmas season is nearing its end, and the power of Santa Claus is indeed unmatched. Nicholas's dreams sell like hotcakes and they run out of stock, unable to meet the demand from their core target of kid customers. They're selling a year's worth of inventory compared to other dreams.

Throughout the season, Nicholas comes in and out of the store like it is his home, transporting his stocks of dreams. He continues to create and restock his dreams, but even when piled mountain-high, they quickly sell out.

Today, wearing a big, brazen belt, Nicholas is busy bringing his products into the dream store with the help of his staff. His stubbly silver beard has a breadcrumb dangling from it, quite possibly from his rushed breakfast.

Young customers seem excited at the sight of fancy Christmas wreaths on the dream packages.

"What kind of dream is in this box?" A boy around the age of six in cute pajamas carefully inspects one of the boxes with a spark of curiosity in his eyes.

"What kind of dream do you want it to be?" Penny asks affectionately.

"Umm… I want a dream where my dad plays hide-and-seek with me and doesn't go to his room, even if I ask him to play for the hundredth time."

"Maybe that's the dream you'll have there. Or it might be a dream where you become an awesome grown-up. Santa Claus knows exactly what you like. I'm sure it'll be an amazing dream," Penny kindly remarks, kneeling down to get to the kid's eye level.

"Really? But I always cry… Santa Claus doesn't give presents to kids who cry. That's what Mom and Dad said."

"Don't worry," Penny whispers in the kid's ear. "That's a tactical rumor Santa spread himself to make sure there are no crying kids who don't want to go to sleep."

"Really?" The kid's eyes widen.

"Think about it. If you guys whine about going to bed, you won't be able to buy any dreams from Santa, right? This is just between us, but it won't sit well with Santa if he doesn't sell his dreams during the season."

Penny recalls the fancy decorations and delicious food

at Nicholas's house. It would be hard to maintain such grandeur if his sales slipped during his one peak season each year.

✷ ✷ ✷

With the last round of customers from Samoa in the South Pacific, the last time zone to greet Christmas, the whirlwind season finally ends. Weather has taken a long vacation to spend the end of the year with her family.

"I made this vacation approval software," she'd told Penny. "You list the dates you want to take off and get Dallergut's approval here. But he doesn't know how to use it, even when I specifically made it to make his life easier. So, I do the approval myself. In fact, I changed it to an automatic approval system. If you want to go on vacation, just plug in the dates and go. Dallergut couldn't care less," Weather had added, before taking off.

That is why Dallergut and Penny are now covering the front desk. Nicholas slouches on the empty seat next to them after bringing in the last batch of his dreams.

"Dallergut, any dream recommendations for a good night's rest? I plan to hibernate for a couple days straight. I'm so burned out. My age is catching up with me."

Dallergut picks out several dreams and sits next to Nicholas. Penny takes this opportunity to take a seat as well. Her knees hurt after repeatedly crouching to make eye contact with the kid customers throughout the day.

Nicholas reaches deep into his thick lambswool jacket, which is held closed by a brass belt, and pulls out a big glass bottle. The dark liquid inside is layered with thin ice as if it has been buried deep in the mountain snow.

The three share the exotic, sparkling dark-red drink. The bottle says, "17 percent Freshness added." One sip makes the throat itch but quickly fills the mouth with a refreshed feeling. It is like holding a heavily compressed dawn breeze inside your mouth.

"This is amazing." Penny fills one more cup.

"Right? I think it'd go very well with bacon. That would end my day on a high note…" Nicholas smacks his lips. "Anyway, I've made a good job transition. If I were to do what my great-great ancestors did, trying to get to every house by reindeer to deliver presents myself… Santa Claus would have long disappeared. They have stronger home security systems now, anyway. But today all you have to do is get kids to sleep, and the rest automatically follows. How convenient! Plus it pays well!" He makes a "cash" gesture, rubbing his index finger and thumb together. "In fact, I hear my ancestors couldn't reach as many houses as they liked because of all the costs that went into feeding the reindeer and getting the presents. I mean, I can't imagine how they managed to handle those expenses."

"We are where we are thanks to our ancestors' sacrifice." Dallergut steps in. "And thanks to the sacrifices you make every year, Nicholas. Speaking of which, I feel our sales this year have increased from last year. What do you think?" Dallergut fills his cup.

"Actually, I don't think it was that different from last year. Last year's sales were on another level. But I'm pretty sure I'll still win the Bestseller category in the year-end awards. And you know what that means, Dallergut? That means I would be winning for fifteen years in a row! Fifteen years! What a record, ha ha ha," Nicholas says confidently.

Penny can guarantee Nicholas is right, having watched the year-end awards with her family every year. On top of the Grand Prix, the awards include Rookie of the Year, Best Art, and Best Screenplay, among others.

But there is the Bestseller award, which is only based on sales for December. And ever since Penny can remember, it has always gone to Santa Claus. Of course, Nicholas has never attended the awards himself, because he always disappears into his cabin after the Christmas season. So Penny hadn't known until now that he is in fact the great Santa Claus.

The awardees of the Bestseller category receive grants

from the association in honor of their economic contribution to the industry. Rumor has it that the reward is a pretty good sum of money. Penny now understands where Nicholas's extravagant "cabin" and furniture come from.

"I wonder what I should do with this year's prize. Last year, they gave me ten bottles of Flutter on top of the grant. It helped me wait for my living room remodel to be finished with a flutter in my heart. I was never bored throughout the entire process. I hope they give out Cozy this year as the additional prize—maybe five bottles."

"What would you use it for?" Dallergut asks, curious.

"Oh, my friend, you should use some of the Cozy like I do. Remember how the couch felt at my house? Didn't it feel like something was hugging your body, like you were being protected from head to toe? You just spray Cozy on your furniture. The effect lasts for at least a week. It makes a huge difference when you come home. I finished my last bottle today, but the price has skyrocketed, so I don't dare to buy a new one. It'd be great if they gave it out as a prize this year." Nicholas speaks as if he's already been declared the winner. But Penny thinks it probably is a given that he'll get yet another award this year. Because it is a year-end ceremony, they only take the last month into consideration when giving this award, and there is no dreammaker who could top Santa Claus for December's sales.

Penny thinks it may have been Nicholas's plan all along to sell dreams only in December, with the year-end awards in mind. People may call him cunning, but Penny thinks it's a testament to his incredible marketing tactics.

Soon after, Nicholas gets packed to leave for his "cabin" in the snowy mountain and heads out to his vehicle, which is parked in front of the dream store. The vehicle is flat with an open top, resembling an enormous sleigh.

"Hey, are you planning to screen the awards ceremony at the store for your staff again?" Nicholas asks Dallergut as he starts the engine.

"Of course, if my staff agrees. I plan to invite their families, too. Care to join?"

"I'm too shy around these events. Especially when I'm a leading candidate for one of the awards. I prefer to sit through the ceremony on my living room couch." Nicholas chuckles. "So long, my friend! And you, young lady—great work! Come visit again." Nicholas bids Penny farewell. His sleigh soon disappears down the alleyway, leaving behind a throaty engine sound.

With Nicholas gone to his cabin in the snowy mountain, the dream store spends the last week of the year with very few customers. Penny looks at the Eyelid Scales of the regulars and realizes that even those customers who normally visit on time have been coming later and later. And when they do come, they only skim through the products, barely window-shopping, and often leave empty-handed, saying, "I just want to sleep well." They all have huge bags under their eyes.

"What's keeping everyone up so late?"

"There are a lot of get-togethers around this time of year. They're sad to let the last days of the year pass. So, they spend each day to the fullest, and when they come back home, they go out like a light, you know," says Dallergut, who seems unbothered.

"I don't know about the other floors, but our first floor's sales have dropped significantly. At this rate, Nicholas could easily win for the fifteenth time in a row. He's already sold big time during the Christmas season."

"Well, you never know. A dark horse may appear at any time."

Looking at his face, Penny can instinctively feel something is up. "Is there another dream that sold more than Santa Claus's? Whose dream is it? Do we have a big rookie who I don't yet know about?"

"Certainly not a rookie, but his dreams have always sold well around this time. He came up like a dark horse at around this time of year, thanks to his increasing sales, which are on par with Nicholas's, but he's always been so self-effacing that nobody ever seems to notice. But one thing is for sure: this year will be his year."

"Who is it? Is this someone I know?" Penny's dying to know who Dallergut's talking about.

"Well, how about I drop some hints instead of giving you his actual name?" Dallergut loves to tease out an answer. Fortunately by now, Penny's used to his style, so she indulges him.

"This time of year can seem joyful and glamorous on the outside, but it carries a dark undercurrent of loneliness and emptiness. It shows when you see how desperately people want to make plans and stay out late," Dallergut says.

"Yes, I understand that. I feel pressured to go out and make special plans during the holiday season, doing things I don't normally do. You feel like a loser if you come home early."

"And who do you think gets the loneliest during the holiday season?"

"Singles like me who have no plans but work nonstop," Penny replies. Despite having answered almost too confidently, she secretly hopes this is not the correct answer. It feels pathetic to admit.

"Well, that's not a wrong answer, but it's not the correct one either."

"Then… Maybe the parents? They just wait around for their kids to come home from their Christmas events."

"That's a good guess, too."

"Which means it's also not the answer. This is hard. I need more hints, please."

"Think of those customers who rarely stop by the front desk and just go straight to the elevator for the fourth floor. Does that ring a bell?"

The fourth floor is for nap dreams, mostly filled with the elderly who often take naps, or babies and animals who sleep all day and night. Penny still has no idea.

"Is it too hard? Oh, they're coming now!"

Penny turns to the entrance where Dallergut's pointing. There, a pack of dogs and cats come swarming in. An old dog wags his tail next to a shabby young man with a backpack as big as his body. The backpack has various pouches dangling from it, making him look like a peddler.

"Animora Bancho! I've been waiting for you."

"Hello, Dallergut. You too, Penny. How've you been?"

"Good to see you, Bancho!" Penny's excited to see him.

"Manager Speedo from the fourth floor called me and said they are out of stock, so here I am. You won't believe how hard he's been pushing me…"

Penny's more in awe of Speedo's ability to wrangle Bancho.

"So I quickly made more dreams. It's been ages since I came down from the mountains; I almost got lost. If not for these boys, I would've gone the wrong way."

His animals rub against his body and whimper, and Bancho pets them affectionately, as if he understands them. He mutters, "Oh, is that so? I hope my dreams are helpful to you."

"Do you know what they're saying?" Penny asks as she helps him put down his backpack.

"Not entirely, but I can understand them if I pay close attention," Bancho replies, blushing bashfully.

"Wow, really? That's amazing!"

Penny looks from Bancho to the dog clinging to him. He's old and losing his fur in some places, but his tail is wagging.

"I remember this dog from my first tour of the fourth floor. He was in the nap dream section, checking out the 'Playing with Owner' corner. What did he just tell you?"

"He said, *It's late and my family hasn't come home yet.*"

The old dog gives a sad look and whimpers again.

Bancho nods and pets him gently. "He's worried that something bad might have happened to them. Don't worry, Leo. When you wake up from a good night's sleep, they'll all be back home. Do you want to try this dream I brought? I made more of that 'Taking a Walk' dream you love! You pups can all take one. I have plenty!"

Leo and the other animals gather around Bancho's backpack. That's when Penny realizes whom Dallergut was referring to when he talked about the dark horse.

It was an old but clean apartment for a family of four. The middle-aged couple was out at a dinner party, and their daughter and son were also out at holiday gatherings. Leo, the family's old dog, who had turned twelve that year, was fast asleep, alone inside the dimly lit house.

During the day, Leo lay flat on the balcony, patiently awaiting his family's return. Holding his ragged stuffed toy in his mouth, he went from room to room, making up for the walk he didn't get to go on. As the day turned dark, the dim lamp automatically lit up, but it still left the house hollow, and the only thing Leo could do was sleep. Fortunately, he dozed off more often as he got older. He was fast asleep now, dreaming Bancho's dream. Thanks to "Taking a Walk," Leo was running around and having a good time.

Beep, beep, beep, beep.

Just then, there was the sound of the digital door unlocking. But Leo didn't budge, deeply immersed in the dream. Half-awake, his eyes fluttered open reflexively, but he immediately fell back to sleep.

It was the four family members, who had coincidentally arrived back at the apartment at the same time.

"Oh, look at you guys, coming home before midnight? That's new," the dad said to his kids by the shoe closet.

"I know, right, honey? I thought you guys would be out later than us. Look at you, all grown up now," the mom chimed in.

"We still stay out late, don't worry. It was just, you know, a boring party." The daughter glossed over it, and then without taking off her shoes, she called, "Leo, we're home!"

"Maybe he's mad because we've been out so long. He's not greeting us. Just sleeping."

"He hasn't eaten any of his food." The son turned on the light and checked Leo's bowl. "And hey, don't wake him up. He's deep asleep."

"Okay, okay," the daughter said as she clung to Leo, still with her coat on. "Guys, you should take a look at this," she called for her family, giggling.

"What is it?" The rest of them gathered around Leo. He was lying flat on the mat, his short front legs hovering in the air as if he were running. He seemed to be smiling.

"He must be dreaming of running. Man, this is too adorable!" The son opened his phone's camera to capture the moment.

"His legs are too fragile now. Our cutie-pie must have been dying to run if he's dreaming about it…" The father seemed like he was choking up.

"Oh honey, you get so emotional when it comes to Leo. You were never like this with the kids," the mom chided.

"How about we walk him right now? All of us together. Let's have a quick stroll around the neighborhood."

At the word *walk*, Leo woke up with a jolt. He realized his family was back home; he was beside himself, trotting around in circles, not sure who to greet first, wagging his balding tail as hard as he could.

✷ ✷ ✷

It's the last day of the year. After closing the shop, the Dallergut Dream Department Store staff gather in the lobby to watch the Dreams of the Year awards. The empty displays and cabinets have been pushed to one side to make room for a row of folding chairs brought in from the storage room. The space looks ready for the screening.

"The best way of enjoying the year-end awards is to watch it all together at the Dallergut store!" Motail from the fifth floor exclaims, as he sits in the last row with his colleagues, taking out his supply of snacks. Though they're technically on vacation, they've come to the store to watch the awards together. Some have brought their elderly parents, their kids and cats.

The Leprechauns, who were invited by Motail, are flying around, adding to the commotion. They start singing one of their work songs, one they usually sing while making shoes. Mogberry has to plug her ears. All the food and drinks and merriment makes Penny giddy with excitement.

Dallergut has been struggling to power up the beam projector against the lobby wall for the last thirty minutes. He's wearing his comfortable jeans and long-sleeve T-shirt, the projector instruction manual tucked under his armpit.

"Are we there yet, Dallergut? Do you want me to try? We should hurry, or we'll miss the first categories! I don't want to miss a single moment of Wawa Sleepland on-screen," Speedo says, pestering Dallergut.

"I'm almost done. But why is the screen black?" Dallergut asks, though he remains dead set on finishing the setup himself.

"It's been thirty minutes since the ceremony started, so they should be announcing the Rookie of the Year, then the Bestseller award. We don't need to see *that*, though. It's always been Nicholas," someone says.

Penny starts to feel anxious. She's more curious about the Bestseller winner than any other category. While most people assume Nicholas will win yet again, Penny's been secretly hoping it's Bancho, ever since Dallergut tipped her off.

Of course, it doesn't really matter to Penny who wins, but when she thinks of Bancho's shabby clothes and his hungry dogs, she wants to root for him.

Just then, Penny notices that two of the cables Dallergut has plugged in are in the wrong sockets. While Dallergut is busy rereading the instructions, she pretends to refill his cup and takes the chance to quickly switch the cables.

"I think it's working now, Dallergut!"

"Finally, I did it! See, I'm not technologically illiterate! Weather should've seen this."

Penny snags a seat between Dallergut and Mogberry as the awards ceremony appears on the massive screen. The camera captures a packed audience of well-dressed dreammakers.

Vigo Myers watches from the far corner, downing shots of strong whisky. "I should've been there..." he says, already tipsy.

"Binge drinking with kids around? What's wrong with you?" scolds Mogberry from the front row, as she turns toward Myers.

"What do you know about me...?" Drunk Myers looks like a completely different person.

"Why did Myers give up on becoming a dreammaker, anyway?" Penny whispers to Mogberry.

"That's a question I ask myself, too. I'm also curious to know why he got expelled from college. Regardless, he still could've pursued a career in dream production without a college degree, so why the pivot?" Mogberry wonders aloud. "Maybe if he gets more drunk he'll tell us."

As well-known dreammakers appear on-screen, the atmosphere in the room livens up.

"Did you see that? Wawa Sleepland is looking gorgeous as usual tonight!"

"Keith Gruer got his hair shaved again. Another breakup? Tut, tut."

Everyone adds their own comments as the awards continue.

The camera now focuses on the host onstage.

"Hello to everyone watching us live at the Dream Art Center for the Dreams of the Year awards! The feverish excitement is palpable here. Hawthorne Demona just claimed Rookie of the Year, and she's still crying in the audience. Congratulations again, Hawthorne!" The host applauds toward the audience. "Now, back to the awards! We're running a little behind, but next up is the Bestseller award. Which dream had the biggest sales in December? Will defending champion Santa Claus win again? If so, it'll mark his fifteenth win, an unprecedented record! Well, let's see our nominees first."

The screen splits into four, showing each candidate. Nicholas, who is absent again, is replaced by the big text "Santa Claus," and the rest of the nominees are caught off guard seeing their faces captured on camera.

Keith Gruer, well-known for his romantic dreams, scratches his shaved head with a bashful smile. The fantasy/science fiction dreammaker Celine Gluck is mildly surprised, but quickly recovers as she blows kisses amid an enthusiastic roar from the audience. But the last nominee looks like he has a huge fishbone stuck in his throat.

"Is that Animora Bancho? Unbelievable!" shouts Speedo from his seat behind Penny. He never expected to see Bancho on-screen. Penny's heart is pounding, thrilled to see him nominated like Dallergut predicted.

The host pauses to build the tension, before delivering his lines. "Now, the Bestseller award goes to…"

Penny clenches her fists. *Please, please…*

Dallergut holds his breath in the seat next to her.

"This is incredible. We have a new winner! The award goes to Animora Bancho!"

As soon as it's announced, the room erupts. Penny and Dallergut stand up and cheer.

"Mr. Bancho, please come on up. Could anyone help him? He seems frozen in shock!"

Dumbstruck, his mouth agape, Bancho is forced to go up onstage, but even when he receives the grant envelope, he still doesn't seem to believe what's happening. His oversize suit looks as though it was borrowed from a thrift store, but he manages to pull it off fine.

"Come on now, Bancho. Your fans across the world are waiting to hear your reaction," the host comically urges him.

"S-sure, of course! Well… This is a surprise. I never thought I'd win this award, even though I did feel my sales had improved significantly this month. But anyway, thank you so much. I especially want to thank my regulars: Leo, Ebony, Lucky, Snowball, Aaji, Charcoal, Mandu, Love, Nana, Choco… I should stop there, or else I could go on and on. To all my furry friends! I know you might not be able to catch this ceremony, but I want to tell you how incredibly happy I am to have met you all. I got the prize money!" Bancho holds up the envelope. "This will help me create many more great dreams for you! So please stay healthy, eat well and sleep well. Stick around with me as long as you can!" He seems much more at ease now that he's addressing his animal friends. "It was just a few years ago when my only dream was to have my products on display at the Dallergut Dream Department Store. I can't believe I'm receiving this award. Hey, Dallergut, are you watching? Thank you so much for believing in me and offering me a contract when I was a nobody."

People in the store whoop and scream at the mention of Dallergut.

"Wait, no mention of me?" Speedo balks.

"And… To everyone's Santa Claus, Nicholas. I'm sure you're watching from home. You know, I've always wanted to make the world a better place for children and animals. And then I met you. You're my role model. You've already achieved the very goal I'm pursuing— creating dreams that make kids happy. I looked up to you so much that I even settled in the snowy mountains, determined to create dreams for animals. I wanted to follow in your footsteps. I know it's you leaving the food and firewood at my front gate every morning. If it weren't for you, I'd have starved to death or been frost-bitten by now. Dearest Nicholas! Allow me to take this award from now on, and you should start aiming for the Grand Prix next year! I'll stop by your cabin with some wine. Oh no, the host says I'm out of time now."

The audience bursts into laughter.

"So that's it for my speech, and I'll be dismissed. Thank you, guys, and Happy New Year!"

He makes his way back to his seat, amid genuine cheers and applause.

After Animora Bancho's unexpected win, the Dallergut staff play guessing games for the remaining categories. Motail gets in a drunken discussion with Vigo Myers about potential winners.

"Who will win the Grand Prix of the Year? Most likely one of the Legendary Big Five, I guess?"

"That's a given. My bet for Best Art is on Sleepland's 'Living Rainforest,' so it would be either Kick Slumber or Yasnoozz Otra for the Grand Prix. It's always been a competition among the five...no one else has ever won."

"Why not Babynap Rockabye or Doje?" Motail suggests.

"Doje has never come to these awards, plus he didn't create any new dreams this year. As for Rockabye, she's already won the Grand Prix a couple of times with the same repertoire. This year will be tough for her. I'm betting on either Kick Slumber's 'Flying as an Eagle on the Cliff' or Yasnoozz Otra's 'Putting Yourself in Someone Else's Shoes Part Seven: Living as a Bully of Mine for a Month.'"

As Vigo Myers predicted, the Best Art award goes to Wawa Sleepland's 'Living Rainforest.' The screen shows an edited version of Wawa's award-winning dream in all its otherworldly beauty. The color scheme's wondrous spectrum changes according to the time of day and the direction of the sunlight. Penny gets why the judges' votes were unanimous.

"If I were a judge, I wouldn't give the Best Art award to the *dream*. I would give it to Sleepland herself. She is way more beautiful than her work," says Speedo, mesmerized by Sleepland as her face fills the entire screen. He moves right in front of the projector to be closer to her.

"Get out of the way, Speedo. We can't see a thing!" shouts drunk Myers. "And would you please tie up your hair? It's going all over the floor."

Best Screenplay goes to Hawthorne Demona, who also won Rookie of the Year. She's at a loss for words and cries, overwhelmed by another win. Her dream, "The Lonely Crowd," is about being treated as invisible. It receives wide acclaim from the judges for its social commentary on the attention-seeking mindset by locking the characters in extreme solitude and amplifying their emotions.

Apparently, that is not how Myers sees it at all. "Total nonsense. Those kinds of dreams have been around since I was, like, three. What a sneaky move to copy an existing, hoary dream with a slight title change. She may have fooled the judges, but she can't fool me!"

The ceremony is nearing the end, with only the last award, the Grand Prix, remaining. Motail roams around, asking people whether Kick Slumber or Yasnoozz Otra will win.

"Your turn, Penny. Who would you vote for?"

"Is there any prize if I get it right?"

"Oh, right! I forgot this is your first time. Yes, we give out a gift card to all the staff members who guess the winner of the Grand Prix correctly. Dallergut's treat, basically. You can get any dream in the store for free. It's the highlight of the year-end awards!"

"Really?" Shocked, Penny looks at Dallergut, who sits next to her.

"Last year, over a hundred staffers got the winner right, and I almost started the new year bankrupt because they only picked expensive dreams…" Dallergut recalls, looking somewhere between wistful and despondent.

Penny thinks hard and eventually writes down "Kick Slumber" on the paper Motail handed out. Lots of staff write down unfamiliar names. Mogberry selects a particularly obscure dreammaker, Chef Grang Bong.

"Mogberry, who is Chef Grang Bong?"

"He's the owner of a dream store I frequent. He exclusively makes and sells eating dreams, and he was very helpful when I was on my diet. Thanks to him, I could eat as many french fries as I wanted in my dream, without ruining my meal plan. Though the one drawback was that I woke up much hungrier! But he's the best for me! Wait, they're announcing the Grand Prix winner now!"

After a special performance, the host, now in a new, fancier suit, comes up onstage for the Grand Prix winner announcement.

"I have two nominees for the Grand Prix of the Year in my hand. What dream will take the honor of best dream of the year?"

The host slowly takes out a piece of paper from the envelope. "These are the two nominees. Let me get to them right away! The first nominee is Kick Slumber for 'Flying as an Eagle on the Cliff'! And the second nominee is Yasnoozz Otra for 'Putting Yourself in Someone Else's Shoes Part Seven: Living as a Bully of Mine for a Month'!"

The second-floor staff all stand up to applaud Vigo Myers, whose prediction was right on point. He shrugs contentedly, his lips twitching.

"But there's only one winner of the Grand Prix award!

I can already hear you shouting the names. Everyone watching us live, who do you think is the winner? Let me hear you scream the name!"

As soon as the host says that, everyone in the store chants "Slumber" or "Otra." Penny joins in, shouting, "Slumber!" The tension in the room excites her. It's like a play-off sports game.

"And the Grand Prix of the Year goes to…"

The host waits for a beat, and the crowd's chanting grows faster, morphing into one giant crescendo. As the tension rises, he peeks in the envelope, takes a big gulp and shouts the name.

"Kick Slumber's 'Flying as an Eagle on the Cliff'! Congratulations!"

Cheers and sighs explode all at once. Penny hugs other Slumber voters and excitedly spins around with them in circles. Some are strangers to Penny, but they're all united by the shared moment of joy.

Motail cheers, swinging his coat up in the air. Speedo leans against the wall in disappointment, having voted for Yasnoozz Otra. The cheers echo outside the dream store, and the entire street celebrates.

Penny notices a pack of Noctilucas outside the window, running around and screaming with joy too. No doubt Assam's among them. He's an avid Kick Slumber fan.

From the audience, Kick Slumber shares a congratulatory hug with Yasnoozz Otra, on his way to the stage. The camera catches Wawa Sleepland in tears, as excited for Kick Slumber as if she herself had won.

"Slumber's dream ingeniously captures the realistic sensation of an eagle—the desperation it faces at the edge of a dangerous cliff, and the dramatic moment when it spreads its wings and soars high! Congratulations, Mr. Slumber!" The host reads his lines as Kick Slumber approaches the stage.

When the dreammaker finally reaches the podium, the room goes silent. Glowing tan skin, thick eyebrows, sharp jawline and pitch-dark eyes. He's standing on his signature crutches. He was born with a short right leg that only reaches the knee.

"Thank you very much for this award. I have the greatest honor yet again," Slumber begins. His voice trembles, but everyone is too captivated to notice. "I've made a lot of boring speeches already, so this time, I'd like to share something personal. Forgive me in advance if it's still boring."

Motail, who's been roaming around chitchatting, quietly takes his seat.

"As you can see, my mobility is limited," Kick Slumber continues, pointing at his right leg with one of his crutches. "When I was thirteen, my mentor taught me how to create animal dreams for humans. As some of you may already know, this was how my dream 'Crossing the Pacific Ocean as a Whale' came to be."

The audience hoots in recognition.

"People praised the dream, claiming it allowed them to experience true freedom. But it got me thinking about my own freedom. I can walk, run and fly in a dream unencumbered, but when I wake up to reality, I can't do any of those things without support. Yet the whales roaming the ocean are not free on land, and the eagles soaring through the sky are not free in the ocean. Freedom comes in different shapes and forms; every living thing is granted limited freedom." Kick Slumber glances into the camera lens then out across the room.

"What makes you feel you're not free?" he asks to the breathless audience. "Whatever it is that has you bound—whether that is a place, a time, or an outdated belief around a physical disability… Please don't dwell there. Instead, seek out the things that do bring you freedom. And during that journey, you may feel like you're at the edge of a cliff. That's how I felt this year. I had to fall off the cliff a thousand times—maybe tens of thousands of times—to perfect this one dream. But the moment I decided not to look down and resolved to kick off the cliff and fly, I was finally able to complete this dream of an eagle soaring high in the sky. I truly hope that you will also have this moment in your life. It would be my dream come true to have my dream inspire you in any way. Thank you again for this award."

A storm of applause.

Kick Slumber closes his lips tightly and nods at the host in gratitude for allowing him to complete his long speech. He looks back to the camera. "I would also like to take this time to thank someone special who has helped me along the way. Thank you, Wawa Sleepland, for contributing the scenery in my dream. You have gifted me with the deep ocean, the expansive sky and the warm field. I dedicate this award to you, my love, and I hope to continue our partnership for as long as we can."

"My, what a lovely couple!" Mogberry exclaims.

Speedo slumps down in front of the big screen.

"Everyone, this year's Grand Prix winner: Kick Slumber!" The host takes the microphone. "Tonight should be an unforgettable night for Slumber fans everywhere. Thank you for staying with us throughout this long event. I'm Bamady Han, and I'm honored to have been your host. Happy dreams in the new year, everyone!"

✸ ✸ ✸

The ceremony is over, but the Dallergut Dream Department Store is still hopping. To everyone's surprise,

Mogberry is spiritedly talking with the Leprechauns. "Oh my God, you're touching up my hair? That's so sweet!" she says, gratefully looking at her hand mirror as some of the Leprechauns fly around her and tidy up her baby hairs. "My hair looks so dark and shiny! All my baby hairs are gone. Thank you, guys!"

Penny think she smells shoe polish coming from Mogberry's hair, but she turns a blind eye. She has been meaning to find the right time to ask Vigo Myers about his college expulsion, but he's sound asleep, drunk. *Maybe next time*, she thinks.

Dallergut quietly rises and starts counting gift cards for the winners of the bet. Penny realizes he has more gift cards than there were winners. It seems everybody will go home with their hands full.

The roaming Noctilucas, seeing the lights from the store, come in, along with some customers, to check out the commotion. It's the most festive night, and the one-minute countdown to the new year is about to begin.

Thirty seconds… Ten seconds… Five seconds…

"Three! Two!" shouts Dallergut. "One! HAPPY NEW YEAR!"

For Penny, this last night of the year, spent with her beloved community, is everything.

SEVEN
YESTERDAY AND BENZENE RING

It was early Friday morning, and the man sat at his desk, looking from his computer monitor to the rust-caked window. He slid it open, desperately hoping for some fresh morning air as he rubbed his dry eyes, trying to wake himself up.

People were bustling out of the nearby apartment complex on their way to the subway station. The man's home was in the slanted alley on the first floor, in a sunken space resembling a basement. It would have been better if it were truly underground. At least then his rent would've been cut by fifty thousand won.

"Hey, on my way to work now. Any plans tonight? It's Friday."

The outside world was alive with the energy of the

approaching weekend, the noise of people making plans carrying along the streets. The man felt hopelessly adrift looking at them through the window.

I'm the only loser here... Locking myself away, making a big fuss about trying to create music... Is my dream bigger than my talent? I wish someone would show me where the line ends between ambition and delusion...

The man had been focusing on composing original music for an audition that he'd barely managed to get. The right song was proving hard to come by.

✳ ✳ ✳

His dream was to become a singer. It was the only dream he'd ever had. When he was very young, he'd signed with a small record company, but his debut fell through when he was in his midtwenties. Time flew by and he was now twenty-nine.

He'd been posting his cover videos on social media; earlier that year, one of them briefly went viral. It had even led to the opportunity to audition for a big record label. But their response after the audition set him back to square one.

"We expected your voice to have more color. How about writing your own songs? We can wait. Consider this another chance."

The man worked part-time jobs, desperate to make ends meet. He wanted to join a composing academy or take lessons to master new instruments, but he had neither time nor money. He asked around and managed to get his hands on some composing software. He installed it and taught himself how to write his own songs.

Some months, he spent more money than he earned; other months, when he tightened his belt, he'd be lucky to save a few dozen bucks. He was trapped on a hamster wheel with no progression.

He made changes to the melody and practiced his original song until his throat burned. He was running out of time to finish the piece before the audition. He just needed one catchy tune, and he felt like he was almost there. So, he'd stayed up all night working on it.

His eyes were stiff and he was hungry. There was nothing to eat at home. The convenience store was just a five-minute walk away, but he didn't like going there during morning rush hour. The thought of being the only one with eyebags walking against the crowd as everyone else hurried to work was revolting.

The man listened closely to the outside bustle. He paid attention to people's footsteps and voices, seeking inspiration for his music, pressing keys similar to each sound on his keyboard.

The man tried to incorporate the voice of the passerby

who'd been talking on the phone as a motif. He wanted to capture the relaxed nature of stable, full-time workers and their excitement for the weekend. Still, the song was not quite satisfying. The pedestrian's anticipation of a restful weekend was not something the man could have. He couldn't even imitate what it might feel like.

The man had decided. He'd weighed the sacrifices he'd need to make to pursue what he wanted. He'd given up an ordinary life because he couldn't give up on his dream. At some point, this earnest desire to be a singer had become an inextricable part of him. He couldn't picture himself wanting to be anything else. And he strived to accept his state of mind as it was.

He continued to work on the music in his cramped room. The secondhand computer sounded like it might burst as it struggled to run the heavy software beyond its capacity. Frustrated, the man shut down the music-making program, then opened the search engine and typed the first thing that came to mind.

When you're frustrated.

When you feel like you're nobody.

When you have a dream but no talent.

There were similar questions but no satisfactory answers.

Do we have to be successful? If you've done your best, isn't that already a success?

It wasn't what he wanted to hear right now.

The man typed "inspiration" into the search engine, hoping that it might ignite something within him.

Inspiration—the process of being mentally stimulated to do something creative.

It was what he'd been longing for all this time, but didn't yet have. He knew inspiration likely wouldn't come to him through a search engine, but he was desperate. He changed his search keywords to more concrete things.

How to get inspiration.

As soon as he clicked "search," a list of countless videos and web pages followed. He started scrolling, struggling to fight off exhaustion. Then his eyes stopped at one particular webpage.

Geniuses Who Gained Inspiration from Dreams

According to a biography of Paul McCartney and the Beatles, McCartney composed "Yesterday" in a dream. As soon as he woke up, he went straight to the piano and played the tune before he forgot it. He was concerned, however, that he may have listened to another that had stayed in his subconscious and manifested in his dream.

"For a month, I went to everyone I knew in the music industry to check if they'd heard the same song before. I felt like I was returning a lost item to the police station. I had no one claiming this song for several weeks, and so I decided I could claim it as mine."

That was how a true classic of our time, "Yesterday," was born—out of a dream...

The structure of benzene proposed by the German chemist August Kekule von Stradonitz is another widely known case of a dream-inspired innovation. Kekule dreamed of a snake biting its own tail, which in turn inspired him to think of the benzene ring. It was a move away from the conventional theory that molecular structures are in linear forms...

Extreme drowsiness poured over him. The more he tried to focus on the letters, the heavier his eyelids became.

He dozed off on his computer desk. Just as he fell asleep, melodies filled his mind, and he drifted away wrapped in a cloud of music.

✳ ✳ ✳

The dream store staff is lining up at the front desk with their gift cards, ready to trade them in for a free dream.

"Everyone, please keep in line and let us know what dream you want. We have to complete all purchases before lunch. Do try to select dreams that are reasonably priced—you guys work here, after all," Weather instructs from the front desk.

"What should I get?" Penny asks her coworkers as she waits in line.

"Here's a tip. If you have no idea what to buy, just follow Motail," Mogberry says. Motail's near the front, jockeying for position with Speedo.

"Speedo, I was here first."

"I'm sorry, but I just hate waiting in line. Can I please just cut ahead?"

"That's nonsense! Please go back to the end of the line." Motail won't budge. His long hair swings sideways as Speedo keeps pushing against him.

"Those two are at it again," Penny observes, but then returns to the point, asking, "But what do you mean, always follow Motail?"

"Penny, have you ever wondered how those two got hired here?"

"I mean, I see how fast and efficient Speedo is. I heard he's the only one here who can process nap dreams inventories at volume." At first, Penny didn't quite get how Speedo became the fourth-floor manager—but then she saw him in action. No matter how much work he has, he always manages to finish everything by the end of the day. There is no such thing as overtime in Speedo's world.

"How about Motail?" Mogberry asks.

"Motail…makes great sales. He's a natural marketer."

"It's not just that. I'm pretty sure he's siphoning off more than he's selling. And, of course, Dallergut knows."

"Then why is Dallergut still letting him work here?" Penny asks.

"Because every dream Motail decides to either sell or siphon off has turned out to be a hit! He finds pearls in the mud. Last year, he chose a new dream from an unknown dreammaker. People scoffed at him that he was putting his gift card to waste, but later, that dream became a huge success."

When it's Penny's turn, she heeds Mogberry's advice and asks for the same dream as Motail.

"I'm sorry, Penny, but that one's out of stock," Weather says apologetically. "Why is everybody asking for the same thing as Motail?"

"Oh no… Can you tell me what dream he asked for? Just curious."

"It was called 'Fantasy Elevator.' Basically, if you think of a place you want to visit, you board an elevator and its doors open to that desired place. It seems like excellent value—if you can focus during the dream."

"What a bummer it's out of stock. Sounds like people into lucid dreaming would love it. I'll just take a 'Meeting a Celebrity,' then." Penny can't wait to take a day off and sleep in late to enjoy the dream.

"That's a wrap! Let's all get back to work, everyone!" Weather shouts as the staff scatter back to their floors. "Hey, Penny," she adds. "Can you look after the front desk for a minute? I have to stop by the bank on an errand for Dallergut. You should be good on your own by now, right?"

"Yes, of course!" Penny says assuredly.

Thirty minutes pass, and confident Penny has disappeared. Instead, there's sweaty Penny, struggling with a male customer who's giving her a hard time. He's been bickering with her, groaning that he's searched everywhere, on all the floors, but still hasn't found the dream he's looking for. Weather's errand is running long, and Dallergut has an off-site meeting with a dreammaker. Penny's now facing her worst predicament since she started the job.

"I'm sorry, but there's no such dream here, sir."

"Please, could you check again? I'd like an inspiration dream. I really need one—right now." The gaunt man is desperate. His skin is rough and his hair bushy, showing signs of fatigue and malnourishment. His pleading, intense eyes are barely staying open. "I've heard stories about the Beatles and Kekule's benzene ring, and that's why I'm here! They all said they drew their inspiration from a dream. Are you not allowed to sell to people like me? Is it because those kinds of dreams are too expensive?"

"I'm sorry, but I have no idea what you're talking about—what is Beatles? And what is the benzene ring? Please don't get me wrong, all our payments are processed afterward, so the price will never be a reason to refuse selling our products, sir."

Penny looks through the store's brochures but can't find any "inspiration dreams." Are there hidden dreams that Penny isn't aware of? She contemplates for a moment, then calls all the floor managers for help.

"I've been a dream salesman my entire life, and I've never heard of such a dream. I know basically every dream in the world. Paul McCartney? I'm sure he may have visited us before, although I wouldn't remember. I don't really indulge in small talk with customers. But one thing I can guarantee is that there is no such dream anywhere in the world," Vigo Myers tells the man firmly.

"By the way, you look unwell. Are you okay?" asks Mogberry, concerned.

"Sir, how many hours did you stay up?" Speedo asks, quickly scanning the man's condition.

"Forty... No, forty-eight hours?"

Everyone shares a deep sigh and sternly says in unison, "The first thing you need is to get some sleep."

The man is in despair, as if his last remaining hope has been taken away.

"What brings all of you here to the first floor?" says Dallergut, taking off his coat as he arrives back from his off-site meeting.

"Well, the thing is…" Penny explains to Dallergut what's been going on. Dallergut looks sympathetically at the customer, who brightens up, hoping he might help.

"I think this might do the trick." Dallergut hands him something. "Please eat it on your way out."

"Will this give me inspiration?" the man asks excitedly.

"Well, it depends."

The man receives it with delight and rushes out of the store, clutching it tightly so no one else can see it.

* * *

The man slept so deeply that when he woke up it was already late afternoon. His neck was sore from lying slumped over his desk. But his mind was refreshed.

He also realized that all the melodies that had once cluttered his headspace were now sorting themselves out and flowing in order. He played the notes on his keyboard, not knowing where they'd come from.

Have I heard these tunes before? Or did I hear them in my

dream? He was unsure. *In any case, I should write them down before I forget.*

The man started filling in the gaps in the melody to complete the song. He had no idea how it came about, but this was clearly the tune he'd been looking for. He was deeply satisfied with how the song turned out. He couldn't wait to perform it for others. Tomorrow's audition would be his first chance.

★ ★ ★

Time passes before the man returns to the dream store to see Dallergut.

"They loved the song. But more than anyone, I loved it. I wrote the lyrics myself, too. I'm embarrassed to say it, but it's based on my personal story." The man is glowing. "I'm recording this week. I wanted to stop by to say thank you. Dreams are a wonder, indeed. It resolved something I'd been wrestling with for so long. I owe you a great deal." The man bows in respect.

"Actually, there's no need to thank me at all, sir."

"Pardon? Then whom should I thank…"

"You should be thanking yourself."

"I'm sorry?"

"I just gave you a piece of Sleep Candy, that was all. You know, to help you sleep?" Dallergut takes out a couple more Sleep Candies and displays them on his palm. "That dream had been in your mind all along."

"Really?"

"*Inspiration* is a convenient word. It suggests that grand ideas might come out of nowhere, emerging across a blank slate. But in fact, a great idea hinges on how much time you spend agonizing over it, and that's what makes all the difference: whether you spent enough time searching for the answer or not. That's the key. My friend, you just stuck around and agonized until you found your answer."

"So, does that mean I *do* have talent? Do you think I can succeed?"

"I believe you know that better than anyone else. I'm no expert. But I do suggest sleeping as much as you work. Especially if you're filling your days with singing. Sleep will help you organize everything that's in your mind."

"Is that so? I still want to thank you regardless. Just for...everything." The man is eager to express his gratitude.

Dallergut's half embarrassed, half pleased. An idea comes to him and he touches his lips. "If you're thankful... Would you let me create a dream based on your story?"

"On my story? What for?"

"Well, I've been talking with a dreammaker friend of mine about our next lineup, and I need some story samples. But we'd need to get your approval to use your story. Of course, we completely understand if you refuse."

"What's your next lineup?"

"It's not set in stone yet, but we do have a working title. It's called 'Lives of Others.' We plan to roll out the trial version first. It's being made by a very talented dreammaker, so I'm really looking forward to it."

"That sounds fun! If my story helps in any way, please go ahead and use it."

"So, that's a yes?"

"Of course! Dreams are so interesting. It's also incredible that the word has a double meaning. Come to think of it, is it fair to say I've found my dream in a dream?" The man giggles.

He's in much better spirits than he was during his last visit, Penny thinks. *Must be that he's getting more sleep.*

He browses the store for a long while and heads out with two short dream products.

"I have a feeling he'll become a regular. I might order a new Eyelid Scale for him," Penny says, as she watches him go.

"You think so? Weather can give you the name of the Eyelid Scale company."

"Sure, I'm on it," she replies.

"And one more thing—can you call Yasnoozz Otra and let her know to start on production for the lineup we discussed last time? She'll be excited to hear that we have the long-awaited sample."

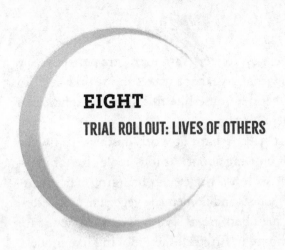

EIGHT

TRIAL ROLLOUT: LIVES OF OTHERS

While out on a business errand, Penny finds herself on the outskirts of a residential village, full of magnificent mansions.

"Yasnoozz says she's completed the lineup sample for our new release. Can you go fetch it for me? You can get some fresh air on the way," Dallergut had requested.

Now, Penny sits alone in the living room on the first floor of an enormous mansion. Built-in lights in the high ceiling cast a warm glow over the room. Through the window, Penny can see a garden with a few abstract sculptures interlaced with vines.

A set of finely patterned navy blue drapes and sheer inner curtains dance in the wind. The house exudes an air of maturity, possibly from a Calm diffuser. Penny thinks its sleekness reflects Yasnoozz Otra perfectly. She wonders how many years of wages she would need to save up to live in a house like this. The thought leaves her ambivalent.

Otra must still be hard at work upstairs. Only the house staff is bustling about. As if to apologize for making her wait so long, they keep bringing her green-grape-ade, egg tarts and homemade vegetable croquettes.

The staff members are as stylish as Otra. They roam around the house in fitted clothes, looking like models. Penny's own outfit feels too loose by comparison, and she tries to pull it taut.

Just as Penny starts to worry that Otra might have forgotten about her visit, a young boy peeks over the second-floor handrail.

"Are you from Dallergut's dream store? Ms. Otra asks you to come up to the second floor!"

There are more than a dozen rooms on the second floor. Penny follows the young boy to one at the end of the hallway. As they approach Otra's office, they pass a woman wearing an achromatic T-shirt and trunk shorts who's just leaving.

"Is she a customer?"

"Yes. Ms. Otra meets with her customers at home in person. Most of her works are custom-made through one-on-one appointments. I believe that was her third meeting today. The client will probably visit a few more times to finalize all the details. Her meeting seems to have run longer than expected. Ms. Otra is usually very punctual."

The boy stops in front of a door with Otra's self-portrait hanging on it. He gives it two short knocks. The black-and-white portrait captures Otra's profile with her eyes closed.

"Here, you can go right inside."

"Thank you."

Penny opens the door to be greeted by Otra. Her hair is shorter than it was in the general assembly.

"Welcome. I'm sorry to have kept you waiting."

"No worries at all. I didn't wait too long. I'm Penny from the Dallergut Dream Department Store."

"Oh, you were at Nicholas's cabin last time. I remember you."

Otra is wearing a blouse with fancy sleeves and high-waisted slacks. Her workroom is filled with various reference materials and photographs. It looks like a movie set, complex yet tidy, with a shelf full of fashion magazines and an impressive display case like those at the store. Penny wonders what dreams they contain.

Otra takes a seat on the couch, crossing her legs, her back against the window. Penny sits on the couch across from her. Otra pours dark roast coffee into her mug from a carafe by the couch, and its bitter aroma settles faintly around the room.

"Would you like some?"

"I'm okay, thank you. Your staff gave me a bunch of snacks and drinks."

"Great. As for me, I desperately need some caffeine. It's been a rough day. I had three customers come by for consultations this morning."

"Yes, I saw a customer leaving as I came in. I heard she's met with you a couple of times already."

"Yes, my customers mostly struggle with denial. Same with that lady. She's wasting her days away, comparing her life to others. And it's gotten worse." Otra runs her long fingers through her short hair. "I need a couple more sessions with her before diving into the work, because I'm still not fully clear on what she really wants. I'm trying to figure out what kind of help I can offer." She sips her coffee. "Anyway, how was the trip? Hope it wasn't a rough ride."

"No, not at all. I had a pleasant trip, thanks to your vehicle service. I really appreciate it," Penny responds, but she keeps getting distracted by the thick doors of the display case. They're overdecorated in a rococo style, but there's a digital thermometer attached to it, which looks out of place. It must be part of a built-in air circulator, since Penny hears a low buzzing sound. *The dreams inside must be priceless*, she thinks.

"What a case, right? Want to take a look inside?"

"Can I?" Penny jumps at the chance.

"Of course!"

Otra approaches the case. Inside, there are densely wrapped dream boxes. Others are stored separately and affixed with padlocks. Penny has heard enough about Otra to know that she finds as much enjoyment in her dream collections as she does in her fashion collections.

"I got all these from auctions. They're all rare products." Otra opens the display case and takes out one of the locked boxes. "This one's more than thirty years old. Made by my late mentor."

"Won't it have gone bad by now?"

"No, it should be fine. I've never seen my mentor's dreams go bad. Plus I've put great care into preserving it."

"What kind of dreams did your mentor make?" Penny can't believe she's having a personal conversation with a legendary dreammaker. She tries to maintain her composure, even though she's starstruck.

"She created dreams that let you live other people's lives. An incredible woman. She always emphasized putting one's heart and soul into each dream. I won't even come close to accomplishing half the things she did in my whole life."

"But you're one of the Legendary Big Five. I'm sure your mentor must be so proud of you," Penny praises.

"That embarrassing adjective, 'legendary,' is nothing more than a gimmick created by the association to sell more..." Otra blushes. "Do you want to know how long the runtime is?" she asks.

"Yes—how long is the dream?"

"Seventy years. *Seventy*. Can you believe it? She poured her entire seventy years of life into this dream, until her last breath. Then she passed it on to me. Whenever I miss her dearly, I think of opening it up and dreaming it. Then I could relive the moment I first met her or gain insight into the processes that made this masterpiece possible."

"Then what's holding you back from dreaming it?"

"Because the dream will be gone afterward. For now, I'm just content that I can keep it in the display case under my care. And this other dream below—I barely managed to get my hands on it at an auction. It is Nicholas's debut work. He made it when he was very young. He probably has no idea I have this. Penny, I recommend developing an interest in bidding on dreams. They have a higher return on investment than artwork," Otra advises. "Now, shall we get down to business?"

She removes a small box from deep inside her desk drawer and places it between them.

"This is a trial version I made with the sample you sent the other day. For the title, I'd like to keep Dallergut's suggestion—'Lives of Others.' I love it."

"Who would the target audience be? Dallergut never gives me any information…" Penny is flustered.

"Call me old-fashioned, but this generation compares themselves with others too much. I understand it is inevitable to some extent." Otra shrugs. "But if it gets to the point that it affects your life, it's a serious issue. This is for them." She gently pushes the small box toward Penny.

"This will be a huge hit. That's a given, because you made it," Penny says.

"Who knows, it might flop and no one will buy it. I'm keen to see how Dallergut will market this. My dreams don't usually sell well," Otra says modestly.

"No way! We can't get enough of your work."

"One of my works last year, 'Living as a Bully of Mine for a Month,' was well received by the critics, but the sales were actually low. Who in the world would really want to live as their bully? I should've given it a less direct title." Otra chuckles heartily. "Without ads, my work doesn't sell well. That's why we put so much money into TV commercials and outdoor billboards. Had I spent less on ads, I would've gotten new curtains for my office already. Anyway, since we haven't done any promotion this time…you and Dallergut have a critical role in selling this dream."

Penny senses the gravity of the task. "Sure, I've got your back!"

"Thanks." Otra grins. "By the way, we should mark the box, so it doesn't get mixed up with others." She starts writing something on the boxtop: *"Lives of Others" (Trial Version)—created by Yasnoozz Otra.*

Like a special agent with a mission, Penny puts the small box deep inside her bag, feeling determined. She rushes out of the mansion, heading straight back to the dream store.

* * *

It was one of those listless Sundays. The man slept in. By the time he ate a quick meal and caught up on his laundry, it was already late afternoon. He lay down on the sofa, watching a rerun of a music program. Each episode, three new guests were interviewed, then each performed their songs in the form of a mini concert. As the man tuned in, he was glad to see that the last guest in the lineup was the writer of the very song he'd been playing on loop.

"Our last guest is so popular that a number of artists

are lining up to collaborate with him!" The host gave an introduction before inviting him onstage. "Of course, that includes me! I'm dying to ask for his number after this show," the host added playfully. "Holding the top place in the charts for two months in a row, everyone, please welcome Do-hyun Park!"

The man had seen the singer in person a few days ago at the tumbledown multiunit building on the corner of a street he passed on the way to work. The singer had lived in the same city for a long time, and word had spread that he was moving out. When he did, people swarmed his home to get a glimpse of him, including the man. The thought that a celebrity had been living so close by was astounding to him.

"You must be so busy these days!" the host said, greeting the singer.

"Yes, it's been hectic. But I do enjoy it."

"Has it sunk in yet? Your massive popularity?"

"No, not really. I still can't believe it." The singer smiled widely.

"These past couple of months must've been a big transition for you. How has it been? Did you ever expect your first song would be this successful?"

"Things have changed so much for me. I had been toiling in obscurity for a long time, and I never thought my music would do this well. But I was very happy with how the song turned out after I wrote it. And I think that's important."

"You must be fielding a lot of phone calls from people trying to reconnect with you."

"Yes, it's surreal. I still feel like I'm in a dream just being here. I watched your show every week, never daring to dream about making an appearance here myself. I thought I would've been content just to have any small stage to perform."

He must be so happy to have such a glamorous life, the man thought, his eyes locked on the TV screen.

Recently, the man had grown bored with his own life. He had a girlfriend and a stable job, but every day was the same. Waking up, getting ready for work, going to the same office, meeting with the same people, talking about the same things over lunch, considering himself lucky if he didn't have to work overtime, and then hurrying back home. The lightning-fast weekend, before the cycle repeated, was what kept him going, making it an almost bearable torture.

That singer's life will now be filled with new people and new experiences. How would it feel to be loved by thousands? How amazing that must be! His music royalties must be huge, too.

Lately, whenever celebrities appeared on-screen, the man would look up their age and achievements. He felt relieved if they were older than him, but if they were younger or around the same age, he'd grow disheartened.

How come our lives look so different at the same age?

He didn't necessarily have complaints about his life. He just wished his life were more special. Hearing people say that some are born unique, or destined for the extraordinary made him wonder if he was just born average, adding to his sense of disappointment.

A flood of thoughts coursed through his mind as he lay on the sofa with drooping eyelids. *No wonder they say you get sleepier the more you sleep. I just woke up not too long ago…* Then, he fell into a deep nap, with the TV still on.

✳ ✳ ✳

The man is browsing the nap dreams on the fourth floor of the Dallergut Dream Department Store. One employee is following him around, making it hard for him to window-shop.

"Good ones quickly run out of stock, especially for nap dreams. More people nap nowadays, and today is a weekend. I'd recommend taking whatever's left, rather than searching aimlessly. They'll all be gone soon." The long-haired employee in a jumpsuit keeps pressing him.

The man seeks refuge in the corner marked "Short Trip in Daily Life." But the fun travel packages are already sold out.

"How about this one, sir? It's my personal favorite."
The employee keeps pestering him. The dream he's
holding is "Flying to Work." The "flying" part sounds
nice, but "work" rubs him up the wrong way.

"I would rather not dream about going to work on
a Sunday."

"What? No way!" Speedo leaps in shock. "I mean,
in this dream you can get to work in just three minutes
with no traffic!"

"If you go to work early but can't leave earlier, what
good is that…?" The man trails off.

"What I mean is that you can get things done fast,
whether it's commuting to work or otherwise. You don't
get it, man."

"Oh, well. No, thanks. I'll just forgo the dreaming
and get some good sleep instead." The man doesn't want
to be bothered anymore. He turns his back on Speedo's
pouting mouth and takes the elevator down to the store's
exit. It is Dallergut who stops him just as he's leaving.

"Sir, may I ask what length of dream you're looking for?"

"Roughly fifteen minutes. I'm just taking a short nap."

"Fifteen minutes. That is… Perfect. And you're looking for something different, right?"

"How did you know? My daily life is boring, nothing's

fun. It's all the same, every day," the man says quickly. It's as if he's been waiting for somebody to ask him.

"Then how about 'Lives of Others' (Trial Version)? This one here. It has all the know-how of Yasnoozz Otra's time magic. You will technically dream for only fifteen minutes, but you will have a very long and special experience." Dallergut enthusiastically promotes the dream. "And since it's a trial version, we'll only take half the price."

"'Lives of Others'? It sounds interesting! What kind of life? Whose life is it?"

"You'll know more when you're in it, but it's about the life of a famous singer, who rose to stardom overnight. I'm sure you're familiar with him."

One particular singer comes to mind. "I actually dozed off watching him on a TV show! What a coincidence!"

"Well, maybe it's not a coincidence," Dallergut says mysteriously.

❋ ❋ ❋

In the man's dream, he's in a small room. He's tired from a lack of sleep and experiencing a severe migraine from artist's block. The room is cramped. A loud motor noise echoes from the old computer as it attempts to render heavy software. Frustrated, the man shuts down the program.

He's living a simple life. He no longer desires money or fame. All he wants to do is finish the song to his satisfaction.

The man opens the window screen to let in as much fresh morning air as possible, rubbing his dry eyes to stay awake.

Neighbors from the nearby large apartment complex head to the subway station, passing the corner of the alley where he lives.

"Hey, on my way to work now. Any plans tonight? It's Friday." The office worker on the phone is undoubtedly the man himself, but the man in this dream does not recognize him.

In the dream, days go by filled with self-loathing from unemployment and guilt toward his family. His distorted pride makes him avoid calls from friends and family who ask after him, which in turn only makes him feel more pathetic. Wash, rinse, repeat.

That is how the man spends fifteen days inside the dream.

✳ ✳ ✳

The man woke up from his nap. He had only slept briefly. The same music show was still on, and the last singer was sharing his concluding remarks before his final performance.

"The last song contains all the emotions I felt during the last eight years of being an unknown singer. I would pretend everything was fine on the outside, but when I returned home, I had to confront all these real emotions. Looking back, I can't imagine how I withstood all that."

For eight years? The man thought of the anguish he experienced for fifteen days inside his dream. He couldn't possibly imagine the depth of the pain the singer must have endured for eight years.

People head in the same direction
Against the current, I head to the convenience store

As the singer calmly delivered his performance, the man saw a reflection of his dream state. A self-portrait strangely overlapped with the singer on-screen.

Beams from the setting sun burst into the living room. The man winced. Today, the sunset felt stronger than the sunrise.

He looked around at all the things inside his apartment that were shining in a new light against the sunset. Usually, this time of day, especially on a Sunday afternoon, was the gloomiest hour for him. This time, it felt different.

* * *

"What do you think happened to the customer who bought the trial version? The payment hasn't arrived yet," Penny says.

"Enlightenment comes with time," Dallergut replies, tidying up a pack of catalogs on the front desk.

"What kind of payment will arrive for a dream like 'Lives of Others'? I sometimes feel jealous or insecure when I look at other people's lives. Other times, I feel relieved or better about myself." Penny thinks of different situations. She remembers feeling jealous when her classmate got a job in a major dream store before her, or when her friends' families seemed better off. She'd also felt a sense of superiority after seeing a kid working at a loading dock on the outskirts of the village, and she was embarrassed for having felt that way.

"I believe there are two ways to love your life, Penny. The first is to work hard to change your life when you feel unsatisfied."

"That seems about right." Penny nods.

"The second option may look easier, but is actually more difficult. And even if you do change your life through the first option, you must ultimately get through the second to be at complete peace."

"And what is that?"

"To accept your life as it is and be grateful. It's easier said than done. But if you can do it, I believe you'll realize that happiness is just around the corner." Dallergut speaks slowly to underscore his point. "I believe our customers will choose whichever of these two options fits them. Then, their precious emotions will arrive as their payments."

"I have a feeling it'll take a very long time," says Penny.

"And we can definitely take however much time we need. Then we can roll out the official version of 'Lives of Others.'"

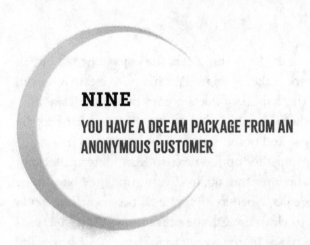

NINE

YOU HAVE A DREAM PACKAGE FROM AN ANONYMOUS CUSTOMER

After a wave of customers passes through, work dramatically slows down, and the staff at the Dallergut Dream Department Store enjoys some precious downtime. Weather hosts a tea for everyone in the first floor lounge.

"If only Dallergut spent more money on the staff lounge and his office," Speedo grumbles, taking up all the space on the sofa for himself. He's reading today's newspaper, while inhaling at the speed of light the cake Penny bought from the dessert shop across the street. The leather sofa is patched and worn, the old-fashioned chandelier missing half its crystals. The broken light accentuates Speedo's custard-yellow jumpsuit.

"I feel like I can finally breathe again," says Mogberry. "My hands were shaking. My body was screaming for sugar." She's smiling as she enjoys the last bite of her marron cake. Speedo licks his plate clean and even scrapes the last bit of buttercream out of the cake box. When there's nothing left to eat, he spreads open the newspaper and obliviously sprawls across the sofa.

Penny sips her coffee next to him, determined not to clean up after him again. Every time they have these snack breaks, Speedo always eats the most but never bothers to clean up. On the other hand, Vigo Myers sits with his hands tented, ready to fold down the boxes and toss them away at any moment.

"By the way, is Dallergut still with his customers?" Weather asks. Her straw is too slim for her smoothie, which frustrates her.

"Yes, he refused the marron cake, which is his favorite," Penny responds. "Apparently, he has a VIP customer; someone I've never seen."

"Ah, it must be for a delivery service," Weather says, as she takes out the straw and starts using a spoon.

"A delivery service? Do we offer that?"

"Oh my, you still have a lot to learn!" Speedo chimes in. "It's a service for patrons who schedule a custom-made dream for another customer, and Dallergut delivers it for them at a particular time."

"I had no idea we offered that kind of service."

"And when these dreams are complete, Dallergut carefully piles them up in his office like a shrine," Speedo responds, his eyes still fixed on the newspaper.

Penny recalls the pile of boxes she almost threw away one time. "Oh—you mean that tower of boxes in his office? But there must be some misunderstanding. The production dates on some of those boxes are from more than a decade ago."

"No, they're the correct ones. They're supposed to... Oh my! I must buy this!" Speedo jumps up from the sofa, still holding the newspaper in his hands. "This is a perfect one-piece! And not too tight, it seems... I was starting to get bored with my jumpsuits, but this one's perfect."

"What is it? Do they sell clothes in newspapers now?" Myers asks.

"Look at this guy's clothes." Speedo spreads out the newspaper on the table for everyone to see.

In the newspaper's black-and-white photograph, a man, pictured from afar, sits on a rock in a navy robe. His hair is tied up in a bun.

"Look at this outfit. It would make going to the restroom so much easier. I'm going to buy a similar outfit right now. Weather, let me use the computer at the front desk for just a minute!"

"Wait, that's Doje. He's wearing a robe, but there's a hanbok underneath, Speedo. You'll get yourself in trouble if you just wear a robe!" Weather shouts, but Speedo's already gone.

Penny finishes reading the article in the newspaper that Speedo left behind.

Celebrity Spotlight—Doje

According to the polls conducted by *More Interpretations Than Dreams*, the most popular among the Legendary Big Five is Kick Slumber. Over 32.9 percent of the responders voted for Kick Slumber, partly due to his romantic acceptance speech at last year's year-end awards.

Yasnoozz Otra, Wawa Sleepland and Babynap Rockabye take third, fourth and last place respectively, separated by a narrow margin. Most unexpected is Doje's second place ranking. He hasn't been active in the dream scene in the last decade, but his presence remains strong. What's his secret? This author set out to feature Doje, secluded deep in the mountains.

Doje adamantly refused to be interviewed. At our request for a message to give his fans, he said, "Stay as far away from me as possible." And with that, he disappeared beyond the waterfall.

"Come to think of it, I've never seen him around during my time here. And I've been here for about a year now," says Penny.

"Even I only saw him just once," says Myers.

"Doesn't Dallergut do business with Doje?"

"Of course he does! He always stops by to see Doje whenever he goes out for off-site business."

"Wait, really?"

Just then, an internal phone in the lounge rings. Penny quickly picks it up.

"Hello, this is Penny from the first floor."

"Oh, it's you, Penny. I've been looking for you since you weren't at the front desk. Is teatime over?"

"Hi, Dallergut. Yes, we just finished. The cake was so good… You would've loved it. Anyway, did you need something?"

"I need some help in my office. Would you mind coming over here?"

"Sure, I'm on my way!" Penny hangs up.

"Dallergut must trust you a lot. He doesn't ask anyone for that kind of help. Go ahead and lend a hand," Weather says, quickly adding, "Oh, and please refrain from having unnecessary chitchat with the customer. You have to make her feel at ease as much as possible."

Penny arrives at the office to find Dallergut waiting for her with a middle-aged, hollow-cheeked woman. The woman is wearing a set of wide-legged pure white pajamas. Usually, pajamas give off a warm and cozy vibe, but there's something eerie about hers.

"Thanks for coming, Penny. Please, have a seat."

Penny sits next to the customer. *What's he going to ask me to do?* As the customer sips her tea, Penny notices her scrawny knuckles clutching the mug. The woman, Penny realizes, is wearing a hospital gown, not pajamas.

"Penny, could you please write down everything the customer says? I could use an extra hand, so I don't miss anything." Dallergut passes her a pen and a notepad. "Now, to whom should this dream be delivered? I did some research and found that all your family members are our customers. We'll have no issues getting the dream to them at the right time."

"I'd like to send it to my husband and my daughter."

"Okay. Any others you wish to send it to?"

"My parents… Yes, I should send it to them, too."

The customer takes another sip, then her lips contort as she shifts her gaze toward the wall. Penny realizes she's holding back tears. But Dallergut doesn't make any move to comfort her, so Penny also decides to leave her be. There must be a reason Dallergut isn't reacting. Penny focuses on taking notes.

"What would you like the story to be? You can choose the setting and situation. Here's our brochure for your reference." Dallergut hands her an instruction catalog designed to help people customize their dreams. The customer browses through it for quite some time.

"I guess home would be good for the setting. Wait, no, that would be too…unbearable."

The customer seems to have trouble choosing the setting. Penny doesn't understand why her home would be unbearable, but she doesn't interrupt her. She recalls Weather's advice—no unnecessary chitchat.

"If you would allow me, may I offer some recommendations?"

"Yes, please. This is my first time having to do something like this, so it's hard, ha ha. That does sound awkward, right? There's *only* a first time for this kind of thing."

With the customer's approval, Dallergut flips the catalog to the last page. It has a list of background photos: a tall, dense forest, the terrace of a castle right beneath the star-studded sky, a view of Earth from outer space. Most are scenes from nature. Penny instantly knows who the creator of these backgrounds must be.

"These are from Wawa Sleepland's dreams!" she blurts out with admiration, forgetting her determination to keep quiet just seconds ago.

"Sleepland is a famous dreammaker, as you can see from our employee's reaction. You can rest assured of the quality."

Dallergut's clearly giving this customer the best possible service, letting her choose from Wawa Sleepland's backgrounds and even allowing her to pick the story. At first glance, it doesn't seem like this dream could be profitable.

"I see. It'll set us at ease if we meet at a beautiful place. I'll take this." The customer chooses the lush forest. "But would it be possible for you to add some white zinnias to this forest? It's my favorite flower."

"Of course, you've got it. We can add much more than 'some.'"

Penny notes the customer's requests, picturing a forest full of zinnias. "It'll be a truly magical dream!" she says, excited.

"Thank you," says the customer, who seems to feel much better.

"Now, on to the story then. Let me know if there's a particular situation you wish to have or certain words you wish to say. We've already gathered enough data for your mannerisms, how you speak and act, and so on, so there's no need to worry on that front."

"Well… I'd like it to be as natural as possible. Asking how things are, or having casual daily conversations."

"Such as…?"

"Such as…asking my daughter if she's dating someone, or if she still takes out all the cucumbers from kimbap like a baby. You know, the usual motherly nagging you'd see in daily life. And to my husband, I used to tell him to label the wool detergent and the liquid fabric softener, so they don't get mixed up. I think these kinds of daily chats would be enough, but are they too bland? Maybe I should take out the nagging, especially since we'll be seeing each other for the first time after all these years, right?"

"No, I actually love it. Should we also add some greetings to your parents' dreams?"

"To my parents… I would just like to say I'm sorry, and that's it."

Dallergut's busy hand comes to a halt over his notepad. "If there's nothing you wish to say in particular, a lot of our customers say things that will comfort the recipient. At the end of the day, it's your call, of course, but I'm afraid an apology may not necessarily put them at ease. Would that be all right with you?"

The customer agrees. "I see—that's a good point. Yes, let's just tell them not to worry about me, and that I'm doing well."

Penny diligently revises her notes. There's something sorrowful about the calm conversation between Dallergut and the customer.

"Great. I think we're about done. I just have one last question. When would you like for us to deliver it?"

"I'm not quite sure. I'd defer to you to watch them carefully and find a good time. Not too soon, though, you know. Give them enough time to settle. But not too late, either, so they don't hold it against me."

"That's perfect timing. Ma'am, you can leave it to us now."

"I'll trust you guys. And… Thank you so much."

"Thank *you* for choosing us. Have a safe trip back and sleep well." Dallergut respectfully sees her out.

After the customer leaves, Dallergut rolls up his sleeves and starts cross-checking his notes with Penny's. Penny has a mountain of questions, but decides to wait for him to sort out the notes first.

"You seem quiet today, Penny. I thought you would ask questions. That's why I called for you," Dallergut says, peering at her over the notepads he's holding.

"May I?" Penny asks. She's been waiting for the chance.

"Of course you may."

"There's something odd about all this…including the dream the customer just ordered. I've never heard that we deliver dreams for other customers, much less create them. On top of that—"

"On top of that?"

"She seemed unwell. I could tell she was almost crying when she talked about her parents. Like… Yes, like this will be her last time seeing them."

"I knew it when I first interviewed you, but you do

have keen insight. I do have a good eye for recognizing potential!" Dallergut stands up. "I need to deliver two of these dreams today. Can I entrust them to you?"

He picks out two boxes from the piles strewn across the floor. Both are old and are covered in dust.

"Are you sure they haven't gone bad?"

"They're fine. Doje specifically formulates his dreams so they don't expire."

"Doje?" The name catches Penny by surprise.

Doje. The least active of the Legendary Big Five. Secluded and rarely seen in public. He is the creator behind "Meeting with the Dead" dreams.

★ ★ ★

A weeknight at a café. One of the man's favorite things to do was to stop by the café on his way home from work and finish any remaining tasks on his laptop. He liked to feel fully relaxed when he was home. The café was filled with a diverse range of people, from kids, to young adults to people his parents' age.

The man generally ordered an Americano, but with an unusually long line ahead of him today, he felt like reading over the menu. His eyes got stuck on the phrase "caramel macchiato." He'd never liked caramel macchiatos. In fact, he hated them because the name was hard to pronounce and they tasted too sweet.

But it reminded him of his late grandmother.

✷ ✷ ✷

"What do you want, Grandma?"

He remembered bringing his grandmother to the café for the first and only time. She'd said she was thirsty. He handed her a menu, which she struggled to read.

"A-me-ri... What is this drink?"

"A very bitter coffee, Grandma, as bitter as gall."

"Why do people spend money on a drink like this? I hate bitter. I like sweet."

"How about a caramel macchiato? It's the sweetest."

"What does it look like?"

"Here, there's a picture. It's right in front of you."

"Where? Ra-mel...ma? Is this the one? You need to understand that your grandma only learned the alphabet halfway through."

"Look, I'll order our drinks. Why don't you go find us a seat?"

The man grabbed their drinks and saw his grandmother awkwardly occupying the one-customer seat at the window.

He broke into a smile. "Grandma, why take that seat

when there're plenty of comfortable seats here? Come on, let's sit on the couch." The man took her to a wide sofa.

"Wouldn't people hate for an old lady like me to take this couch? Aren't seats like this for people who order more expensive, fancier things?" His grandmother looked around reluctantly.

"We paid plenty, Grandma. Don't worry. And if there's anyone who gripes at you for sitting here, they're the ones with the issue."

"Is that so? I feel safe having you with me."

"Oh, it's nothing." The man felt a bit shy.

"I'm the eldest around here, aren't I?"

"I guess so, but you're the coolest grandma here. Enjoying some coffee time with her grandson at this fancy café."

"You know how to talk like a charmer. Always been so sweet, ever since you were little. It's an inherent gift of yours." The grandmother looked at her grandson affectionately.

He got shy again and changed the topic. "By the way, why'd you learn only half of the alphabet? You might as well learn it all. Only a few more letters left."

"Your great-grandfather wouldn't let me. I just needed three more days of school, but I couldn't go. I was always busy helping him on the farm. Then I got married, raised your father and then raised you. Life kept me too busy. That's why I can't pronounce that cara-mel ma-thing. How funny, right?" The grandmother grinned innocently.

"No, it's not funny. Grandma, I can teach you. You're very smart; you'll learn them in no time. I'm busy with work this weekend… So maybe we can start next week-end."

"That sounds wonderful. My grandson is the best!" The grandmother took a sip of caramel macchiato with her straw. "What *is* this? It's too sweet, my tongue is numb."

"Then try mine, Grandma," the man said, handing her his iced Americano.

"My God, this is too bitter." She frowned, and the man burst into laughter.

"It gets better once you're used to the taste. You just have to come here with me more often."

✳ ✳ ✳

That had been their only time at the café. She died at age eighty-two. She'd lived a rather long life, but it still left him with regrets. The anniversary of her pass-ing was in a few days.

The man ordered a drink and sat at a single-seater table by the window. He thought of his grandmother much more often around her anniversary. Her life growing up had been all for her family, and when she got older, she'd relied on her young grandson. Despite her limited education, she was a wise and virtuous woman who always looked out for him when he was growing up. If he told her how good the soy sauce–braised potato tasted at his friend's house, she'd steam a whole pot of potatoes the next day. If he whined about how his mosquito bite was itching, she'd stay up late to catch the mosquito. The man thought back on all his fond memories of her.

The man looked around the café, taking in the good music, the comfortable chairs, the relaxing mood. He kept thinking back to how his grandmother had looked around this comfortable place, how she alone had felt uncomfortable.

I'm the eldest around here, aren't I?

His grandmother's face, embarrassed but a little thrilled as she peered around. It lingered in his mind. He felt heat in the middle of his forehead, even though he was drinking cold coffee.

He remembered how she'd make him change his clothes if they had the slightest stain. Or how she'd buy him expensive body lotion with long descriptions she couldn't read, when she wouldn't even buy herself a cheap face cream. Every little thing she did was an act of love.

That night, the man lay in his bed, deep in his thoughts. *What was Grandma's life for, when she couldn't enjoy all these things the world now offered, just because she was born too early? What meaning was there in her life?*

A world with suffering and no luxury whatsoever: that was the world she had lived in. Perhaps she was happier now. Maybe that was why she never came to visit him in his dreams.

"I miss you, Grandma."

The man crawled into a fetal position and fell asleep.

✷ ✷ ✷

The couple had a five-year-old daughter who was slow to speak. When other kids were stringing together complete sentences, she could barely utter a few words. As the couple went from one clinic to another, their concerns mounted, but then the child suddenly started talking, articulating what she liked and disliked in full sentences.

When their daughter said, "I love my family," the couple felt like they had just conquered the whole world.

One day, their daughter said, "My head hurts. Can you make it stop?" and that was when their happiness stopped. The daughter was hospitalized soon afterward, and didn't make it past that year.

Some time passed after the daughter left. The couple

was still young, each busy with their own career. Any trace of their daughter had been removed from their home.

When she was alive, the two often joked, "Will we ever see a clean floor again without all these toys everywhere?"

But now, their house was always neat and clean.

They'd gone from being a two-person household to a three-person household, and then back to two. Life moved along. The idiom "Time heals all wounds" seemed to work for them. But every once in a while, they'd bring up their daughter, and end up talking the night away. First with tears, then with more laughter.

The couple no longer shied away from talking about their daughter. At first, they'd avoided the topic, trying with all their might to forget everything, because they thought forgetting was the only way to live, but they soon realized they would never be able to forget her. Whenever they came across toy ads, a yellow bus, a school zone sign, a story about a child actor who was all grown up, or even a new semester or graduation season, they would fall apart.

The wife said she missed their daughter's sleeping face. The husband said he missed the smell of their daughter's soft skin when she hugged him tightly after a bath. Her giggles sprinkled in between their voices, and they reminisced about the funny habits she'd picked up from each of them in equal parts.

Their daughter was forever stuck at five, but they continued to age, and sometimes their lives seemed to pass too slowly. There were moments when both of them secretly thought they would rather join their daughter, before she felt too lonely. But they couldn't bear to share that thought with each other.

At night, they lay in bed, their backs to one another. Out of habit, they saved just enough space for a child to lie down between them. But the gap wasn't big enough to conceal the other's sobbing. They each pretended not to hear.

* * *

Penny starts shimmying as she spots the customers that fit Dallergut's description. She takes out their carefully repackaged dreams.

"Thank you for making it on time."

"I'm sorry? Me?" the man asks. Next to him stands a couple, their eyes puffy from crying. The three of them look at Penny, confused.

"Packages arrived today for each of you. We've been reminding you throughout the day. And you came in at the perfect time."

"What is it?"

"It's a dream. A very precious one. Someone custom-made it for you."

"Who? We don't know anyone who'd send us such a thing," the husband says.

"The sender is anonymous. You'll find out who once you're in the dream."

✳ ✳ ✳

The man sees his grandmother in his dream that night.

The café she takes him to looks similar to the one they visited together, only much fancier. It smells like the house he used to live in with her.

The grandmother confidently orders two caramel macchiatos and casually banters with the cashier. It is like she's a regular.

"Grandma, look at you. Ordering difficult drinks is now a piece of cake for you!" The grandson looks at his grandmother affectionately.

"All thanks to my grandson, who taught me well!"

"I don't remember teaching you."

"You did teach me. Don't you remember? What's wrong with you? You're too young to forget things already!"

"Did I really?" The man looks out the window. He

thinks the view looks a lot like the front yard in the old house they once lived in together, but it doesn't strike him as odd. He just thinks about how much he loves this café. The two share old memories and laughter over coffee, losing track of time.

A café employee offers them a slice of cake. "It's my treat! You two look so happy together."

"Oh, that's so thoughtful of you. Thank you, sweetie." The grandmother gives her a wide smile.

"Lucky me, getting perks just because I'm with you! Guess we should come here together more often."

"No, you should come with your friends. Not with your wrinkly old grandma."

"Now that hurts." The man surveys his grandmother's face and then blurts out the one question that has been brewing in his mind. "Grandma, how would you describe your life, looking back?"

He knows this is probably not the time, but for some reason, he feels like this will be the only chance he'll ever get to ask the question.

"It was a good life," she answers without hesitation.

"It was good? Really? Which part?" He pulls up his chair closer to her.

"When I was a child, I was grateful to have lived with just my family. I didn't have to worry about working for other families."

"How about when you were an adult? I know you went through a lot."

"As an adult, I was grateful to have raised your dad myself."

"..."

"As a grandmother, I loved seeing my grandchild grow up. I prayed so hard that I could live long enough to see you mature and take care of yourself, and thankfully some good god listened to me and answered my prayer! Your granny had such a wonderful life."

She strokes her grandson's cheeks. He remembers her hands being rough whenever she had done that to him growing up, but this time, they are as soft as a baby's.

"At one time the idea of seeing you walk on both feet seemed like something far off in the future. But look at you now: all grown up and ready to lead the way, holding my hand and patiently waiting for me to catch up. My old soul feels refreshed like spring!"

The man suddenly comes to his senses. "Grandma, I think this is a dream, because you're already gone. Is this a dream?" A feeling of dread rises in the pit of his stomach.

"What do you mean, I'm gone? I'm with you, here and now. It all depends on how you see things, isn't that right?"

Tears well up in the man's eyes.

"Oh, Jae-ho, don't cry. Maybe I should've come much later. I can't believe you're still like this after all this time!"

"No, you should've come sooner," the man snaps at her, as he tries to hold back his tears.

"Your granny is doing just fine here. My knees no longer hurt, and I'm also growing my favorite herbs. So, no more crying, okay? I was lucky to have you as my grandson."

"Grandma, don't say that like you're leaving me. Please stay longer, would you? Is your coffee done? I'll go get another one."

The grandmother shakes her head. "It was so nice seeing you, my puppy. You take good care of yourself, okay? Be healthy, achieve as many dreams as possible, and live your life. I know I've achieved mine because I saw you today."

The man senses he's waking from his dream. And he feels remorseful at the thought that asking if he was dreaming might have sped up their farewell.

And then he snaps back to his senses.

★ ★ ★

The man was wide awake, but couldn't get himself to open his eyes. If he did, he feared all the afterimages inside his eyelids would disappear.

He rose from his bed, eyes brimming with tears. He rarely cried, but this time he crouched down and bawled for hours.

✳ ✳ ✳

The young couple are also deep in a dream. They've met their daughter, who has been gone for so long.

The daughter in the dream speaks fluently. "There was sooo much I wanted to tell you guys when I was a baby, but I knew too few words to make up all the sentences."

"Did you? But look at you, you speak so well now. And you're even prettier!"

"You're pretty too, Mommy." The daughter holds her mom's face in her hands and makes an adorable smile.

The couple hug her tight. "We're so sorry you had to suffer your whole life."

"No, I was ninety-nine percent happy and only one percent hurting. And now, it doesn't even hurt one bit!"

"But your life was so short. You didn't get to enjoy anything." Her dad gives her a guilt-ridden, pitiful look.

"No, I'm serious! I only have good memories. And you know, I have a lot of friends and teachers and grandmas and grandpas here, but no one has said they had just good things in their lives. But *I* only had good things! Isn't that amazing?"

"Yes, it is! You're amazing, sweetie. Daddy has only good memories with you, too! My sweet little baby, weren't you sad to be alone, though? Did you miss Daddy and Mommy?"

"I'm fine, because I have a really good memory. So even though I can't see you, I have you all in my heart!" The child wiggles herself out of their embrace. "So we can see each other again much later. We can take it slow. Don't you ever think sad thoughts!" she says to her parents, speaking shrewdly while pulling an adorably silly face.

The couple is on the verge of tears, but their daughter's goofy expression makes them laugh. "Okay, we'll take it slow. But we'll definitely meet again."

"Uh-huh. I'll be a good girl until we meet again. I promise!"

The parents know this is all a dream, but they are overwhelmed with joy, as if they really are meeting their daughter. It is rare for them to dream while being aware that they are dreaming.

The couple woke up from the dream at the same time. It was one o'clock in the morning. Barely two hours had passed since they'd gone to bed. They were clutching the tangled blanket between them.

When they fully came to their senses, they lay in bed, silent, interlocking their fingers. They stayed that way for a long while.

✱ ✱ ✱

"Dallergut, how many people preorder dreams on their deathbeds for their loved ones?"

"Many people try to leave dreams behind. So many that there are even stores dedicated to creating just those kinds of dreams!"

"I have to say, every day has been a surprise here, ever since my first day of work. The moment I think I've seen everything, there's always something more surprising to top it!"

"Is that so? What a fun job you have!" Dallergut laughs. "Yes, it is fascinating. Whether they've been involved in a sudden accident or are bedridden from a chronic disease, people who are asleep seem to know by some instinct when their life is coming to an end. Perhaps in that state, without any external stimulation, their primitive instincts become more sensitive."

"Er… Sorry, I'm struggling to follow." Penny picks out the old boxes from Dallergut's office and piles them up alongside the new, clean boxes. "What I do know is that these dreams should be handled with great care.

Although I could never fully grasp what it must be like to leave something like this behind for a loved one."

"People always try to leave messages in any way they can for those who'll be left behind."

"I know this is too early, but it makes me want to plan ahead what kind of message I should leave when I'm gone."

"What a wonderful idea. My message would be to remember me—or to not hand over my store to a random goose," Dallergut says jokingly. "But when you meet these customers, no one cares about their own self-interest. They only wish for the happiness of their loved ones. I guess that's what it's like to leave your loved ones behind. Although I too cannot grasp it entirely."

Penny looks at the old boxes, damp with time, feeling a bit choked up. She wipes every last speck of dust from them.

"Hey, Dallergut."

"Yes?"

"I just wanted to say, I really love my job."

"Me too," Dallergut says frankly.

Just then, the door flings wide open. It's Vigo Myers and Weather, both in latex gloves, along with Mogberry, holding a new marron cake, and Speedo, who seems to have been dragged along.

"You should've asked for me if you had things to

clean!" Myers looks a bit hurt, but he can't hide his excitement at the prospect of cleaning the boxes.

"I bought you another cake since you missed our party and couldn't have any. Looks like everyone's just about wrapping up with work. How about we finish cleaning up and have some sweets?" Mogberry says, holding up the cake box. Her hair has now grown long enough that there are no more baby hairs sticking out from her ponytail.

"Let's hurry up then," says fleet-footed Speedo, already moving the boxes.

Later that day, toward the end of her shift, Penny is looking for a space on the shelf to put the new Eyelid Scale that has just come in. It's been two whole months since they ordered this customized version. There's one opening way up on the shelf; Penny can hardly reach it, even with a ladder. She carefully puts the scale up there and gently strokes the eyelid-shaped weight with her fingers. The dial trembles and stops between Conscious and Sleepy. After that, Sleepy slowly turns to Asleep.

Penny climbs down the ladder and looks outside to see if her customer is coming. Assam is walking by and waves at her. Finally, her customer walks toward the store from afar. The door opens.

"Welcome!" says Penny. "We have amazing dreams in stock today!"

EPILOGUE 1
VIGO MYERS'S JOB INTERVIEW

Vigo was stiff as a post in front of Dallergut. Dallergut had given him a Calm Cookie, but Vigo's mouth was too dry, and he didn't dare eat it.

"You're shaking, kid. No need to be. We'll just have a little chat, and it'll be over. You can relax, cool?" Dallergut comforted the grown man in his midtwenties. He guessed his nerves might have something to do with what he'd seen in Vigo's résumé. "Is it because you think your college expulsion will be a sticking point? That no matter how great you do in this interview, you think I'll reject you?" Dallergut asked, looking at the résumé. "Do you really think I will disqualify you immediately for that, when you had the highest score in the entrance exam? I thought my questions were hard, but you got them all right. Throughout the entire decade I've been in this business, you are the first to get a perfect score."

"Questions like those are not hard at all," said Vigo in a faint voice. "What's hard for me are situations like these, where I must talk about myself." He hung his head, fidgeting with his dirty nails. He looked unkempt for someone at a job interview. It was like he'd dragged himself there, but lacked the zeal to groom himself.

"I see that you don't want to talk about the expulsion, and I understand. Still, it's inevitable that we have to discuss it. I'm obliged to verify if a person I'm hiring has any criminal history," Dallergut said adamantly.

"I didn't commit any serious crime!" Vigo said, looking Dallergut straight in the eye for the first time. "I just didn't know much about the rules. And it was just that one time. One mistake. I swear."

"So, what happened?"

Vigo twitched his lips, reluctant to open up, keeping Dallergut in suspense.

"It's okay. Don't overexert yourself. You can skip this interview if you can't talk about it. If you really want this job, I can find other ways to verify your history. I can make a phone call to your adviser myself."

"N-no, that can't happen. Okay, I can explain."

Vigo took a deep breath. "I was working on my graduation project," he began.

* * *

"Vigo, have you found a partner for your graduation project yet?" asked a fellow senior who was passing by.

"Yeah. Just got one, and they finally said yes."

For their final project, all seniors had to interview a "real customer" and create a dream for them.

Over the last month, Vigo had camped out every day in front of the Dallergut Dream Department Store. He would beg anyone passing by, "Would you be my partner for my graduation project?" only to be rejected with a look that said, "You're crazy. What's wrong with you?" as everyone went about their business.

After exactly one month, a girl about his age approached him. She was wearing baggy ivory pajamas. "I can be your partner for your graduation project."

"Really? Thank you!"

"I've been watching you here every day for the last month. I don't know what motivates you, but you seem very dedicated."

Her response was totally unexpected. *How can she possibly remember everything that's happened here for a month? She, an outsider?*

"How did you…?"

"Will you keep a secret?" The girl looked around

and then whispered in his ear. "I'm a lucid dreamer. At a very high level, too."

Vigo was shocked. "You can come here at will through a lucid dream? I've never seen such a thing!"

"Yes, when I'm asleep, I can go anywhere I like. And I remember everything that happens there. Amazing, right? So, how can I help with your graduation project?"

The two met every day in front of the Dallergut Dream Department Store on the pretext of working on his graduation project. They talked about lucid dreams and shared stories about where they lived, losing track of time.

It was only natural that Vigo developed feelings for her.

"I want to invite you to my graduation project presentation. I created a dream I want to share with you. But a lot of people will be there. You should wear a normal outfit when you sleep that night so you won't get caught."

But she didn't show up that day. And he never saw her again, which was a clichéd ending for this type of story.

✶ ✶ ✶

"So I started presenting my dream without her. But then there was a problem," Vigo continued.

"What was it?"

"I put myself in the dream." Vigo lowered his head.

"Oh no, you foolish kid." Dallergut sighed. "You're never supposed to be inside customers' dreams and interfere in their lives. Especially when that customer is a lucid dreamer. It's dangerous."

"I really had no idea. I was book smart, but I didn't know there was such a rule in school." Vigo's eyes were pleading innocence. "So afterward... I'm sure you don't need me to tell you what went down, but my professor was furious about my graduation project and held a disciplinary committee. I told them the truth, but I got expelled. And the record remains with the association, so I can't even pursue a dreammaker career... I ruined everything."

Worried, Dallergut looked at Vigo, who was worn out and scruffy. "Did you apply here hoping to run into that girl? This is where you two first met."

Dallergut had seen right through Vigo's intention, and it left the young man at a loss for any excuses.

"Yes, but that's not all! I do love dreams. I know I'm pathetic, but I still want to work in the dream industry. If I can't... I have no reason to live."

"Nonsense! It's obvious you're still not over her. This is unacceptable." Dallergut was adamant.

"I know I'm being ridiculous. I also know I don't stand

a chance of being with her this way. She can come here to meet me, but I can never go where she is. That was why I wanted to show her the dream I'd made for her. To show that I could come and meet her through the dream I'd created…"

"You can't have feelings for a customer. There have been so many young dreammakers whose lives were ruined when they meddled in romance with their customers, trying to be the 'ultimate woman or man' in their customers' dreams. The dreammakers soon realized that dreams could never become a reality for their customers, and it devastated them so much they lapsed into severe depression…and it always ended with—"

"I will never overstep the line again. All I'll do is wait here! So please…"

"Have you ever thought about why she stopped coming? Maybe she stopped having lucid dreams—or maybe something happened to her. You might never meet her again, however long you wait for her." Dallergut was frustrated.

"It's okay. Ten or twenty years from now, I may bump into her. I just want to tell her that I'll always be here if she ever wants to see me."

A long silence fills in the office.

Frowning, Dallergut looks back and forth between

Vigo and his application. Finally, he said, "Keep it between us."

"Excuse me?"

"Everyone probably knows about your expulsion by now, but never tell anyone why. Understood?"

"O-of course!"

"But I have to say, I'm impressed that a college senior already knew how to put himself in a dream. That's definitely something. Okay, I'll give you a chance. You are dismissed. I have an interview with another candidate…"

"Thank you, Mr. Dallergut. Thank you so much!"

Vigo awkwardly stood up and kept bowing toward Dallergut as he walked backward out the door.

"One more thing," Dallergut added, looking at Vigo's shabby appearance. "Starting tomorrow, suit up nice and clean. You never know when she might come."

Vigo smiled widely for the first time. "Understood! I'll be extra clean. I'll clean up and do laundry… I'll clean your entire store! I'll clean *everything*! Thank you, so, so much!"

EPILOGUE 2
SPEEDO'S PERFECT DAY

"Penny! Wait for me!"

Penny's striding briskly toward the store, swinging her bag back and forth, when Mogberry stops her. She's panting, holding an egg sandwich in each hand.

"I've been calling to you. You didn't hear me?" Mogberry says, handing over one of the sandwiches, stuffed with smashed egg. "Here, I know you didn't have breakfast. Take it."

"Oh, I'm sorry, Mogberry. I must've been lost in thought about what to do after work tonight."

"Welcome to the working life, honey."

The savory smell of egg yolk and black pepper from Mogberry's sandwich makes Penny's stomach rumble with hunger.

"Did you make this yourself?"

"My sister made it. She's a great cook, unlike me," says Mogberry as she takes a hearty bite. "I'm staying at her place until the remodel on my house is finished. I guess I'll see you around more on our commute!" she adds, with an especially adorable smile.

By the time they've finished their sandwiches, they've arrived at the crosswalk in front of the bank opposite the Dallergut Dream Department Store.

"By the way, Penny. You still haven't caught that culprit yet, huh?" asks Mogberry cautiously as they wait for the signals to change.

"What? What culprit?"

"You know, the one that stole one of the two Flutter bottles at the bank when you were on an errand for Weather. When you had just started working here—remember?" Mogberry points to the bank building behind her.

"You knew about that?"

"Of course I did! Nothing goes unnoticed at the store. And we managers have to keep track of quarterly revenues; we should be aware of such matters more than anyone!"

"That makes sense. I thought only Dallergut and Weather knew, because no one else brought it up." Penny's face starts to flush.

"Speedo doesn't know, and I didn't think I should tell him. Given his personality, I could already imagine how much trouble he'd give you for it, so I spared you. I mean, his temperament got the better of him when he was just starting out, making mistake after mistake, you know? But look at him now, so ruthless to others," Mogberry shakes her head.

"Thank you so much. Speedo's always given me a hard time, telling me off at least once a day, ordering me to get myself together, saying that I don't deserve to get paid."

"Just brush it off. If we deducted all the mistakes he made from his paycheck during his new-hire days, he'd have made about half his salary." Mogberry pats Penny on the shoulder.

"The thief must've gotten away with it and disappeared for good, right? It's been nearly a year, and they still haven't tracked him down." Penny looks back at the bank with a sigh as they cross the road. "I would feel so much better if they could catch him. If we're lucky, maybe we could get the Flutter bottle back too."

"I know. It would also help the store, you know. Flutter is hard to come by. But people like him usually operate in syndicates. His gangs are probably committing similar crimes even as we speak."

"I don't think they'll use the same tactic again, though."

"Who knows, they might wait until the scrutiny wanes

and come back. It's always in the last place you look. We have to keep an eye out," Mogberry says shrewdly.

The store is full of energy, crowded with employees just arriving and others merrily finishing their night shifts, along with some customers ready to shop early in the morning. One slim employee is waving his hand at Mogberry and Penny. His ripped jeans expose his knees.

"Hey, Mogberry, you should hurry up. Speedo's been looking for you all morning."

"Speedo? Isn't he off work today?"

"I thought so too, but he's here. I'm heading home. Good luck, guys!"

"Maybe I got his schedule wrong?" Mogberry tilts her tightly ponytailed head.

"Mogberry! Why are you so late? I've been waiting for you! For three full minutes! I've already sorted out new arrivals on the fourth floor and got the preordered pickups ready in the lobby. Can you just double-check the list before you leave? And hey, Penny, it's good you're here. The floor tiles in front of the D-17 pillar on the fourth floor have peeled off, so the construction guy from the next town will be coming in today to fix it. Please pay him out of the repairing expense budget, and don't forget to keep the receipt. It shouldn't be over fifty seals a tile, max, so if their numbers are funky, just give me a call right away. Got it?" Speedo fires off a list of tasks for them before they even have the chance to take off their coats. They frantically take down notes.

"Would you please slow it down a notch? I feel like throwing up the sandwich I ate this morning," Mogberry says, looking nauseous.

"I have the day off today, but I came to work early to finish my part. I can't spare even a minute of my time from this point on." Before he even finishes his sentence, Speedo is already running out the door.

Speedo's plan for today is perfect, even by his own standards. He occasionally takes off on a random weekday, because weekdays off feel even more rewarding than weekends after working every minute and second to the fullest.

Humming, Speedo takes out his notepad to check through his to-do list. First, he has to go to the bank and open a new savings account, one he's heard comes with a high interest rate. After a steep learning curve and a few failed attempts, Speedo has quickly realized that high-risk financial investment is not his strong suit. Once he opens the savings account, he'll buy a sweet red-bean pastry at Kirk Barrier's Bakery at 10:00 a.m. sharp. Then, he will head to the greengrocer's timed sale, which starts at 10:20 a.m. That wraps up his morning plans. After that, he'll head to a tempura rice bowl place that opens at 11:00 a.m. to get his brunch without having to wait in line.

"Wait lists are not in my dictionary, even if it's for a five-star restaurant!" Speedo murmurs to himself, as he takes the crosswalk in front of the store. Then, looking into the bank through the spotless glass window, he covers his mouth in shock.

"Oh, no…"

Based on the data he's accumulated throughout the years, the number of customers in line at the bank at 9:10 a.m. on a weekday is five on average. Today, there are eleven.

"No, this can't be right. By the time I'm done opening my account, it'll be way past ten o'clock."

As Speedo mopes in despair, one great idea comes to him. He enters the back and lies flat on the ground. He starts looking around for any queue ticket someone might have thrown away. After raking around the place, going as far as to search under the water purifier—and tearing his snow-white jumpsuit seams in the process without realizing—he finally finds a ticket. The fifth to the last.

People glance at Speedo, who by now is triumphantly sitting in the waiting room after his bank floor scavenger hunt. But he could not care less.

"Amazing. It's a narrow margin, but I'll still be able to make it in time at this rate."

Yet there's one guy who has been bothering Speedo this whole time. He's in a neat suit conversing with elderly people and wearing kind-looking, smiley eyes.

"Excuse me…"

From a distance, Speedo can't make out what the guy is saying, but he can guess. This man is clearly begging the elderly for their queue tickets so that he, too, can get ahead in line.

"To abuse the generosity of the elderly like that! The audacity! How cheap."

Speedo checks his ticket against the numbers on the counter display. They're taking an especially long time today. If that cheap guy cuts ahead of him, there's a good chance Speedo might have to pass on Kirk Barrier's red-bean pastry. The bakery is so popular that once their freshly baked pastries are ready, they almost instantly sell out. The thought of his plans being scuttled makes him panic.

He stands up and resolutely approaches an elderly security guard, who's dozing off near the water purifier.

"Excuse me, sir? Sir? Do you see that guy over there? He's doing something very fishy."

Slowly blinking his eyes, the security guard scans Speedo up and down, then looks around. "What's fishy about him?" he asks, clearly thinking Speedo seems fishier.

"He's only talking to the elderly. Which means… Um… Yes! Wire fraud! You know, voice phishing, or something like that?" Speedo rambles.

"Are you sure?"

"Yes, I'm sure. Would you please escort him out, as soon as possible?"

"Okay." The security guard turns to the stranger and shouts, "Excuse me, sir!" Surprisingly, the guy gets flustered and starts stepping backward, as if he really had been up to something fishy.

"Security! Security!"

A ruckus ensues as all the in-house security guards swarm the guy. Meanwhile, Speedo contentedly sits at the empty counter, unbothered by the scene he has caused.

"I'm here for the new savings account model you're advertising, with a three percent annual interest rate. Can I open it right now?"

After that, Speedo's day is near perfection. He secures a set of ten freshly baked red-bean pastries and buys a box of carrots for a mere fifty seals at the timed sale. He makes it inside the tempura rice bowl place as soon as it opens, and while the food itself tastes unexceptional, it feels terrific to see the waiting line getting longer by the minute outside the restaurant as he eats.

Speedo clears everything on his list, including filling the air in his bike tires and picking up his clothes from the dry cleaner. He returns home and plops down on the sofa, turning on the TV.

"Oh, I still have time until the 10:00 p.m. show," he says. Pleasantly exhausted, he feels his body growing relaxed and languid. "Maybe I'll have a quick snooze." And he falls fast asleep on the sofa.

✸ ✸ ✸

The evening news is playing on TV.

"Finally, we have good news that a criminal organization behind a systemic pickpocketing on Main Street has been arrested. Their targets were older people or newcomers in the waiting rooms of banks and public offices. They would approach their victims impersonating employees of the institution to put them at ease, then steal their money and valuables… One of them was caught in the act at a bank, committing his first crime after joining the group, thanks to a citizen at the scene who reported him to the police. The frightened criminal admitted his crime, disclosed the organization's base and provided further intel, which helped the police arrest the rest of the perpetrators. The police searched the base and found numerous valuable dream products, including, interestingly, a bottle of Flutter. All the valuables will be identified and returned to their original owners, according to the police. Meanwhile, the brave citizen who first reported the crime to the bank security guard disappeared without a trace. The police plan to reward the citizen, so if you are them, please reach out to the nearest police station…"

Just then, Speedo abruptly wakes up and checks his watch. It is five to ten. He snatches up the remote control to change the channel. Luckily, the commercials are playing before the series. Finally, he crosses off his to-do list for the day, with everything achieved as planned.

"What a perfect day," Speedo murmurs, grinning.

TRANSLATOR'S NOTE

They say that the translator of a book is often the book's biggest fan. I can wholeheartedly attest to that. In fact, I'm afraid this note will look more like a love letter. Let me first have a bite of Calm Cookie to keep my dignity so I can add my two cents as a "dignified" translator, although I know I'll utterly fail.

I immediately fell in love with the book as a reader when my sister introduced it to me (I owe you tons of dream payments, Hasun!) long before it became a million-copy bestseller in Korea. The world-building and the characters are so fantastical yet vividly real that I could immediately picture the novel becoming an animated adaptation. Miye Lee introduces the imaginative world effortlessly in a whimsical and palatable way to a wide readership, and it shows in the way she forms a sentence, sets a scene and tells a story that is both fun and deep. It is unpretentious yet full of life, which I wanted to carry into the translation.

I didn't find it challenging to capture the voice because I felt completely in sync with Penny; I equally marveled at the wide variety of dreams, fangirled over the dream industry people and remain in awe of the technology behind dream payments. I connected so easily with Penny because she is such a relatable and adorable character, and in fact, these traits are shared across all the characters—not a single one is unlikable, and I can't help but adore them. Lee's tenderness toward her characters was something I kept in mind in the translation.

One of the fun parts of translating this novel was coming up with new words and rules for my anglophone audience. My favorite new word is *dreammaker* for *dream director*, echoing *filmmaker*. (Thanks, Hyeyoung!) The original novel uses a word for *dream producer* in literal translation, which doesn't quite capture the creative mind of a director. As for the rules, I found it satisfying to use the present tense for the dream world and the past tense for the real world. It distinguishes between the two, but I also think the present tense conveys a fantastical nature of the dream world that transcends time and memory.